STORM WAVILY AND THE PIRATE KING

a Pirates Ahoy Cozy Mystery, Case 1

VERED EHSANI

STERLING & STONE

STORM WAVILY AND THE
PIRATE KING

Chapter One

I HAD no idea the cat could talk until I launched my escape plan.

"I hope you realize that's not going to work," the cat announced. He clawed up my curtains, collapsing onto my windowsill to recover. Huffing, he waddled toward me. His tail — the only slim part of him — swished with all the self-importance a cat can possess.

"You have no idea what works and..." I paused and studied my stepmother's pet. He was a handsome, plump, pompous creature with long, silky black fur. He would've made a perfect familiar for any self-respecting witch if not for his paws. They were all white. "You can talk!"

The cat sat in front of me, tail curled neatly around him. His eyes glowed yellow, and his nose wiggled with disdain. "Humph! Clearly. But can you listen? Probably not. You've been spending too much time with humans."

"You mean my father and his wife?"

He shuddered. "An infectious lot if ever there was. You're practically one of them now."

I bristled at the suggestion I was human. I certainly

looked and sounded like one. But that was as far as it went. I lifted my chin. "I'll have you know I'm a witch, and not just any. I'm the granddaughter of Penelope Evian Puddlewick, Grand Dame of the Wavily Clan, and a member of one of the most important families in the witch world. You, on the other hand, are a mere cat."

"Which goes to show how little you know. Clearly you've been contaminated with unsavory notions after a lifetime of frequenting the home of the human you refer to as *Father*." He sniffed, then began licking one of his front paws.

I decided the best course of action was to ignore the pesky feline. Besides, a talking cat wasn't that impressive, at least not for witches. The surprising part was that no one — including my powerful grandmother — had identified the cat as a potential familiar instead of a mere non-verbal house cat.

The cat stretched, bounced onto my bed, and flopped down. "She's set traps, you know. Grande Dame Puddlewick knew you'd try to sneak away."

"I'm not sneaking. I'm leaving."

"In a sneaky way."

"I'm quite aware of what my grandmother is capable of, cat." I double-checked the contents of my bag. Was I missing anything? I felt like I was. Something important—

He hissed. "My name isn't *cat*. That's what the human female calls me. An insult to the feline race everywhere. How I've suffered in silence."

"I'm sure. I suppose I'm ready to go now."

I surveyed my bedroom one last time. I was sorry to have to leave it. But even more wretched was the arranged marriage Grand Dame Puddlewick insisted I enter.

"A fine match," she'd declared. "He comes from a distinguished lineage almost as exalted and ancient as ours,

Storm. And he's a noble. His family's acceptance of the union is nothing short of a political triumph. Yes, he shall do nicely."

I wasn't opposed to marriage in general, just this specific one. I was a witch, not a mere woman to be married off at the convenience of her family. I wanted to marry for love, not for political and social maneuvering, even if it did benefit my family.

That aside, Queen Victoria was well established on her throne. Didn't that account for something? If the greatest monarch of the greatest empire of the world was a woman, then surely the plight of women everywhere — witches or humans — should likewise improve? The queen held sway over the lives of millions. So why couldn't I decide with whom to produce offspring?

Alas, Grand Dame Puddlewick wasn't so enlightened.

The Grand Dame of the Wavily Witch Clan and permanent member of the European Witch Council had very different ideas. Traditional ideas. It was she who insisted on locking me and my younger sister Misty in the dungeon for a month after we released a basket of toads into the kitchen. She made it clear she was punishing us not for the crime of disrupting the kitchen but for being caught.

Nor were we allowed to refer to her as Granny, Grand-mother or any similar term of familiar endearment. We had to call her by her title. She was the most witchiest witch I knew of.

I was looking forward to my new life, one free from her domineering rule. I had a plan, and a decent one at that. And I wasn't about to deviate from that plan by a smidgeon, regardless of sentimentality or the dubious advice of a fat cat.

I still hesitated.

Was this confusing mess of emotions what my mother experienced when she left us to join a circus?

I pushed the question into a mental box labeled *Do not open on pain of death* and closed the lid. It didn't matter what my mother thought or felt when she ran away. She made her choice. My father — a human through and through — made his and married another human.

My stepmother wasn't a bad woman. She was just... well, *human*. Grand Dame Puddlewick hadn't approved and immediately moved in to ensure that Misty's and my training continued in the witch way.

"Aren't you going to take this?" The cat nudged the chicken egg housed in a small wicker box on my bed.

"Oh! Yes. I almost forgot it."

"This is why you need me to accompany you."

"Out of the question. I can't take you. That would be stealing."

"You can't steal what nobody owns. And I belong to no one."

"I don't really like cats."

"That's all right. I don't like people. I'm coming with you."

"Who are you to say so?"

"An excellent question. Allow me to answer." The cat puffed out his chest, tipped his chin up, and stated, "I am Sir Dedrick Bartholomew Pocock O'Doherty the Third, descendant of the Egyptian cat goddess Bastet. You may now bow before your superior. Or curtsy. I'll accept either as homage to, and worship of, my lofty station. Proceed."

"Hmm. I shall call you Pooky."

The cat's whiskers whipped upward. "I beg your... How did... Blasphemy! That sounds *nothing* like my name, you hairless primate."

"You don't really expect me to call you Sir Dedrick

something, something the Third. I can't remember that many names at once."

"I expect exactly that. My name is distinguished, regal and full of historical significance."

"Your name's longer than you are."

Pooky's jaw dropped, and his whiskers quivered. "Beware, witch. I've suffered in silence long enough. I shall never forget this outrage. I'll shed a fur ball in your tea when you least expect it. It's what cats do as a second resort."

"If you say so."

"Do you want to hear what we do as a first resort?"

"No." I checked the window latch, searching for any sign of tampering.

Grand Dame Puddlewick had been quite thorough in locking all possible escape routes. And I didn't doubt Pooky's assessment. She almost certainly had set traps. She wasn't above using spells, curses and the occasional bear snare if someone tried to defy her orders. Her lightning curses in particular were legendary.

But I was prepared. After all, I was a member of the Wavily Witch Clan. A water witch, and one with a decent amount of talent, even if I was still in training.

I still needed to be careful. Humans hadn't entirely abandoned the unsavory habit of persecuting any woman they suspected of witchcraft or intelligence. It wouldn't do for any of them to actually *see* me perform a spell.

To be honest, I was more worried about being caught by Grand Dame Puddlewick. Another stint in the dungeon was not in my plans. Neither was marrying Lord Percival Paaveling Wavily Moats, a toad of a warlock. Rumor had it he was something of a ladies' man and had adopted an unseemly number of human habits and fashions. That being the case, he probably only bathed once a month. I assumed his smell was as abhorrent as his reputation.

Pooky plopped on my pillow and clawed at it. "Do you want to hear how I was knighted? It's a marvelous tale of tragedy and triumph."

"Now's not a great time. I'm trying to run away. It's what young ladies do as a second-to-last resort. Do you want to hear what our last resort is?"

"No. I wouldn't open the window if I were you. And I thank the cat goddess I'm not."

"Why?"

"I don't want to be a primate, especially a female one."

"I mean why not open the window?"

The cat shrugged. "Feel free to do so, if you wish. After all, it's the closest to the tree outside your room. Correct?"

"Obviously. That's why I…" I paused.

Pooky snickered. "Obvious to you. Obvious to the Grand Dame."

"Hmm. I suppose you're right."

"Was there ever a doubt?"

"For a creature who claims to be a descendent of a goddess, you're rather rude."

"Of course. You're my inferior. Try the other windowsill. No, not in this room. In your sister's."

I hesitated. I'd hoped to avoid seeing Misty. She was much younger than me, a child by both witch and human standards. And I didn't want her creating a scene, which she'd do if she found out I was leaving. She was a soft-hearted, sentimental sort, the poor thing.

"I'll wake her."

"I doubt it. I once dangled a live mouse above her face, and she didn't stir. I suppose I'll have to do all the thinking for us. Follow me." Pooky slid backward off my bed, leaving scratch marks on the blanket, and shambled toward my door.

"Grand Dame Puddlewick'll hear me if I go into the hallway," I whispered.

"She'll certainly hear you if you try opening one of your windows. All of London will. She set an alarm spell."

"How have you kept your true identity hidden for so long?"

"Talent. I have many of them, but I won't exhaust you with a full recitation of them. Are you going to open the door, or stand there staring at it?"

"You mean you don't have the talent for opening doors?"

"Humph. Why bother when I have you to do it?"

"Of course. I feel like there's something else I'm forgetting." I paused at the door and stared around my room. The room in which I'd grown up, learned my first spell, set fire to Misty's hair. Fond memories.

Hair.

My gaze settled on the sharp shears on my writing desk.

"Are you always going to be this slow?" Pooky followed me to the writing desk. "We'll never escape at this rate."

"Why do you need me to escape? You're a feline of many talents. All you have to do is go outside and keep going."

"Humph. But who will feed me? Open doors for me? Set out a platter of cream at the appropriate times?"

"Certainly not me." I lifted up the scissors and rotated them. Candlelight flickered on their shiny surface.

The cat nudged my hand. "You don't really mean that, do you? Especially the cream. Life without cream is... There simply isn't life without cream. Imagine life without tea."

"Why would I do that?"

"Exactly."

I grabbed a thick chunk of my hair. It was long and black. Everyone said I was the spitting image of Grand Dame Puddlewick when she was younger.

I frowned at the thought. Looking like my grand-mother sounded a lot like *being* like my grandmother. And that was one woman I didn't wish to emulate.

"Tick, tock," Pooky said.

"Yes, yes. Give me a minute."

A woman's hair was one of her most prized posses-sions. Nobody much cared what was under her lovely locks. Her brain was of little importance in this day and age. But her hair? That was the symbol of beauty, femi-ninity and the ever-important fertility.

"It has to be done," I whispered.

My plan involved pretending to be a boy. A boy could be given useful work. But a woman? An unaccompanied woman on a ship or in a new city was good for only one thing, and I had no intention of cooking for anyone.

I stared at my reflection. My eyes glowed like a cloud-free summer sky after the rains have passed. Still staring at them, I pulled the clump of hair over my shoulder, settled the scissors against it, and squeezed.

The blades *snicked* together. The hair fell loose in my hands. I let it drop. It floated down and settled at my feet, covering the hardwood floor with black strands.

"Don't stop now," Pooky said. "You look lopsided."

I sniffed back a tear and kept chopping until all of my wavy hair was on the floor around my chair. Grimac-ing, I stared at the mirror. I hardly recognized myself. My black hair stood up around my face in jagged clumps.

"I look like a boy now."

The cat snorted. "Not everywhere. And do boys wear nightdresses?"

"Oh! That's what I'm forgetting."

"You're welcome."

I hurried to my wardrobe and opened the bottom drawer. Sifting through the clothes, I pulled out the pantaloons I'd stolen from my stepbrother.

"You're going to have to be better than this," Pooky lectured. "What would people say if you'd wandered outside in a nightdress for women, and a haircut for boys? They would've committed you to the insane asylum."

"It was a small slip-up."

"A small…" The cat coughed, gasped, spluttered, then spat out a hairball. "It's hardly a small anything. These details are critical for our successful escape. I'm beginning to wonder. Perhaps you aren't the best choice of companion, after all."

"Do you see any others lining up to take you away?"

"Good point."

"Turn around. I'm not comfortable with you watching me."

"Hurry up, then." He turned his back on me and began grooming himself.

I hastily changed, pulling on my stepbrother's pantaloons, suspenders and an oversized shirt. The costume hid my feminine qualities reasonably well. I added a long jacket and studied the results. "Much better. No one will notice what I am. I daresay I could fool Grand Dame Puddlewick."

Pooky made a rude noise. "Highly unlikely. No one can fool her."

"You did."

"Naturally. I'm a cat. Can we go now?"

I'd already delayed long enough. If I didn't leave

tonight, I never would. The engagement party was set for the day after tomorrow, followed almost immediately by the wedding. Security would be tight as witches from high-ranking families across Great Britain came for the festivities.

My bedroom door was locked. Fortunately, I'd long ago learned the invaluable skill of lock picking. I'd never told anyone, not even Misty. I was lucky I'd managed to keep this skill a secret.

In a few minutes, my lock pick set had done its work, and I eased the door open. I held my breath, waiting. All was quiet. I stepped into the hallway.

Something screeched underfoot. I jumped away, preparing to kick whatever it was.

"You clumsy female," Pooky said. "That was my tail."

"Then keep your tail out of my way. And keep quiet." I held up my candle, hoping its light was dim enough not to attract attention.

"Come on. We're almost there." The cat meowed and nudged his nose against Misty's bedroom door.

Another door creaked open from around the corner.

Without thinking, I blew out the candle. Shadows descended around me, cloaking me but not nearly enough. If Grand Dame Puddlewick chose to, she could easily use an advanced night sight spell. I'd yet to master it, but she was the master of all things and all people.

"Just getting some water, dear," Father murmured.

"Open the door, open the door, open the door now!" Pooky punctuated his command by clawing at my leg.

"Ouch!"

"He's coming."

I shouldered Misty's door open and slipped inside her room. Just in time. A puddle of light stretched into the hallway as Father padded toward the stairs.

Had I closed my bedroom door?

I gripped the candle tightly enough to squish the wax, scrambling to remember. Had I closed it? If not, Father would wonder why it wasn't closed and locked. Did I dare use a spell to make sure? But any spell strong enough to reach down the hallway would be strong enough for Grand Dame Puddlewick to detect, even in her sleep.

Father's soft humming passed by Misty's door and continued to the stairway.

I exhaled sharply.

"Hurry." Pooky pattered to the windowsill.

Misty's window wasn't close enough to the tree for me to climb down it, but perhaps I could use the drainpipe.

"Storm?"

I almost bit my tongue. Misty's soft voice reminded me of the one thing I would desperately miss.

"Storm, what's wrong?"

"Nothing. Nothing at all. I thought I heard you call for me."

Misty's yawn was loud enough to make me wince. "No. I don't think I did."

"Good. Go back to sleep."

"I'm not tired. Can you get me some water?"

"Make her go to sleep," Pooky said. "Another door opened. I think old Puddlewick is awake."

Misty lit a candle and blinked in the soft glow. "Who said that?"

I sat next to Misty. "No one. No one at all."

The cat hissed. "How dreadfully wrong you are on all levels. I'm hardly a *no one*."

"The cat—"

"Misty, ignore the cat."

The cat's tail twitched angrily. "It's rather difficult to ignore something as magnificent—"

"Please get over yourself," I snapped.

Misty grabbed my hand. "You're going, aren't you?"

I was tempted to lie. But what would be the point? She'd find out soon enough. Besides, I wasn't exactly dressed for going back to sleep. And my hair! "I have to."

Misty's expression hardened a bit. "Yes. That warlock really is a toad. I'll go with you—"

"Absolutely not," Pooky said.

"Unfortunately, I agree with the cat."

"Because I'm correct as usual. It's bad enough I have to babysit one witch. But two? There are limits even for one of my numerous talents."

"It's going to be okay, Misty." My throat constricted as I wiped a tear from her cheek.

"Will you come back and visit me?"

I hesitated. I desperately wanted to say yes. But it was a promise I couldn't keep. So I said the next best thing possible. "I'll try. I promise you, I will try."

She nodded, sniffed back a tear and got out of bed. "Are you really going to climb out my window?"

"That's the idea."

"You're not very good at climbing."

"I'll manage."

"Without breaking a bone?"

"I wouldn't go that far."

"You might need all your bones to get away from here."

"Misty?" an elderly woman called out.

Misty and I froze. Grand Dame Puddlewick was awake.

Chapter Two

OUR GRANDMOTHER'S voice echoed down the hallway and trickled under the door. Even Pooky flinched.

"She's awake," Misty whispered. "And she's coming here!"

"I know! Lock your door." I dashed to the window and peered down. Misty was right. I wasn't going to escape the house with all my bones intact. But turning back wasn't an option, either.

A walking stick thumped against wood as Grand Dame Puddlewick stalked down the hallway. "Misty, who're you talking to?"

"Myself, Grand Dame Puddlewick."

I pushed open the window and tried not to stare down.

"Wait." Misty reached under her bed. "I have something you can use. I've been keeping it for an emergency. We can tie it to my bed." She pulled out a long length of rope.

And for the first time that day, I smiled.

I wasn't smiling a minute later. Climbing down a rope while it swung back and forth across a rough stone wall was not how I imagined my escape. My imagination had seen me gracefully clambering down a tree and leaping to safety.

But now? I was more likely to tumble to the ground and break a vital bone such as my back or neck.

"Can't you keep this thing still?" Pooky screeched as he clawed my back.

"It would be easier if you'd retract your claws!"

"You want applause?" Misty whisper-shouted. "Who'll steady the rope if I clap? Maybe later—"

"Not you, and keep quiet," I cried out.

"If I retract my claws, I'll fall," Pooky said.

"You have nine lives."

"I value each and every one of them."

"You're terribly heavy."

"Are you saying I'm fat?"

"No, but now that you mention it—"

"I'm not fat. I'm fluffy. It's all the fur."

"It may be fluffy, but it's also weighing me down."

The bedrooms were on the third floor. It didn't look so high up from the sidewalk. But I was now reassessing the height as I dangled somewhere between Misty's window and the hard cobblestone below.

Misty peered at me, her face squirreled up with worry. "Grand Dame Puddlewick's knocking on the door. What do I do?"

"Don't let go, that's what!"

"You're almost there." Misty's skin flushed as she attempted to lie.

"I'm going to die," I groaned.

"You'd better not," Pooky said. "I've committed my well-being and care into your primate hands. So unless you can turn yourself into a zombie—"

"She's insisting I let her in, or she'll blow up my door," Misty loudly whispered and retreated from the window.

"Misty, come back," I cried out as the rope spun. My knees banged against the rough wall.

She reappeared. "Can't you jump?"

"Why would I jump?"

"Why, indeed?" Grand Dame Puddlewick stepped up to the window and peered down at me, her nostrils flaring. "I'm tempted to let you succeed in this foolish escape, but I've already sent out the wedding invitations. So you'll have to return at once."

"Jump it is." I let go of the rope.

Misty screamed, the cat howled, and I yelped as I landed heavily on my bag.

"Am I dead?" Pooky asked, crawling out from underneath me. "Tell me I'm not. I already lost one life to the neighbor's manic dog. I can't keep losing lives like this."

"We're alive," I whispered. "We're alive! And no broken bones."

Grand Dame Puddlewick pursed her lips and reached into her pocket. She was about to pull out a small vial of water that all water witches carry with them for emergency use. That meant she was going to perform a spell. I knew by the hardness around her mouth who would be the target.

I stumbled to my feet. My bag dragged heavily on one shoulder, and Pooky hung off the other. I nodded at Misty and started running down the road.

"Faster, witch, faster," Pooky urged. "She has water in her palm. It's starting to glow. Glowing blue steam's rising up—"

"I don't need the details, cat," I said.

"Save your breath for running, not talking."

I pumped my arms, willing myself to go faster. I didn't

bother stopping to pull out my own water vial. Grand Dame Puddlewick was far too powerful for me to take on in a spell duel.

"Come back here at once, or I'll curse you forever," Grand Dame Puddlewick shouted.

"I'm too beautiful to be cursed," Pooky said. "Can't you speed up?"

We were almost at the end of the street. I was fairly confident I'd be safe if I rounded the corner. The stone should block whatever spell she tossed at me.

"I'll find you wherever you go, Storm," Grand Dame Puddlewick shrieked. "There's no point in running. The deal's been made, the wedding contract signed. Resistance is futile. Running away will only prolong your agony."

"I'm not going to lie, witch," Pooky hissed in my ear. "It doesn't look good. Is that blue lightning she's throwing?"

I almost tripped over my own feet. Blue lightning! Grand Dame Puddlewick was deadly serious about stopping me — emphasis on *deadly* — if she was tossing blue lightning at me. Lightning made by a water witch was never a good thing. If not lethal, it definitely inflicted pain, suffering and a curse or two.

I lengthened my stride, more determined than ever to escape.

A lightning bolt flashed past me, exploding into a nearby gas streetlamp. The flame fizzled and sparked.

"That was a close one. It almost singed the tips of my whiskers. It looks like she has more where that came from."

"Not... now... Pooky!"

"I'm merely trying to help. But if you're going to be so ungrateful, I'll keep quiet."

"That would be great."

"You might want to duck."

I hunched over, and another lightning bolt zipped far too close for comfort. My hair frizzled from underneath my cap, and my nose twitched at the scent of ozone.

"Maybe I'm a good luck cat," Pooky said. "It's the only logical explanation why she hasn't zapped you yet."

"Those were warning shots, Storm," Grand Dame Puddlewick said. Magic magnified her voice across the neighborhood.

I reached the corner just as something nipped at my heel. I staggered against the wall, tripped over a small pile of garbage, and tumbled to safety. I remained seated on the damp stones for a moment, catching my breath.

"That was close," Pooky said. His plump body quaked as he pressed up against me. Whiskers jutted out on either side like he'd been zapped by the bolts. "Let's never do that again."

"Storm Puddlewick of the Wavily Clan, return at once!" Grand Dame Puddlewick's voice boomed after me.

"No rest for the witches." I rubbed my heel. Did one of her blue bolts hit me? Was I now cursed?

Pooky lifted his chin. "Pick me up, then. I'm ready to proceed."

"Makes one of us." I scooped Pooky up in one arm and my bag in the other. I hesitated, listening for any sign of pursuit.

Nothing.

Only the soft fizzle of a streetlamp and my raspy breath interfered with the silence. That made me even more nervous. Either Grand Dame Puddlewick was summoning the stableboy to saddle her fastest horse, or she'd hit me with her curse. Or both. And if the bolt had found its mark, she'd eventually find me no matter where I hid.

It was a good thing I'd anticipated this possibility. Now

was the time for the next stage in my master plan. The only way I was going to avoid the whole unwanted wedding fiasco was by leaving not just my home, but my country.

Not that I was particularly attached. The weather was dreadful, and the humans were on the whole a savage lot. Being a water witch, I wanted to avoid being thrown onto a flaming pyre while still breathing.

"I'll have to stay at sea until I find a strong enough anti-curse spell," I decided.

"Why ever would we do that?"

"*I* will do that. *You* can come or not, as you wish."

"Again, why?"

"Water witches prefer freshwater. Salt interferes with spells, especially long-distance ones. It's a good thing my plan includes a trip over the ocean."

"Fascinating." Pooky yawned. "Anytime now, witch."

"Hmm. I'll worry about those details later."

"You mean where we'll find cream for my breakfast? I like the way you're thinking. You clearly have been well-trained."

I started jogging through the quiet streets, praying no one would see me. It was well into the witching hour. Decent, honest, God-fearing people didn't wander around outside at this time of night. Only ghosts, demons and those up to no good came out to play.

"Where shall we live once we've completed our great escape?"

I paused at an intersection. Quiet. I wished I'd thought of escaping closer to sunrise, at the beginning of the day's hustle and bustle. I could easily hide among the crowds of unbathed humans and horse-drawn carriages. No one would notice a modestly dressed young man heading toward the port.

"It's going to be a while before we find a place to settle down, Pooky," I warned him. It was best to crush his lofty expectations as soon as possible.

"You did manage to bring some funds with you, did you not?"

I patted my pocket. "Enough to set up a new life in the New World."

"The New World?"

"Yes. You know. The colonies. The American Republic. I hear they still have wolves and buffalo."

Pooky twisted in my arms and narrowed his eyes at me. They glowed with hostility, brighter and more yellow than the gas street lamps. "Do you mean to tell me we're going to traverse monster-infested oceans surrounded by unwashed sailors? And why would anyone in their right — or even wrong — mind want to live over *there*? Wolves and buffalo. Humph! What a thought."

"It's the only place I can go where I'll be safe from Grand Dame Puddlewick. Especially if her curse hit me. The oceans'll dilute its effect." As if thinking about the possibility aggravated it, my heel started to ache.

"You're serious. You're really going?"

"Absolutely. New World, here I come. That's the plan."

"What's wrong with the Old World? It's true the humans are barely educated and smell worse than their dogs. And don't get me started on their atrocious grooming habits. But at least they have milk cows here. Do you think they have milk cows over there, across an ocean? No, of course not! Do you know how I know this? Because *cows don't swim*! Not for that distance, at least. And then what'll I do?"

"Chase rats, I suspect."

"Chase..." His nose quivered, and his eyes widened until they were luminescent. "I've clearly overestimated you. I don't *chase* anything. Unless it's yarn. I'll lower my standards for a ball of yarn. But that's where I scratch the line. Rats. Humph! Do you know how many diseases those rodents carry?"

I glanced over my shoulder. My shadow stretched out long behind me as I approached another street lamp. "You're welcome to *not* go with me. I'm sure I can manage from here. I've already purchased a ticket on the SS *Cedric* that's leaving this morning."

"What about going up to Kilkenny? It rains a lot over in Ireland. Rain washes away sunshine, so it'll dilute any curse you might've received."

"It has to be ocean water. Salt, remember? Otherwise, she'll find me, then force me to marry that horrible, stinky water warlock she's picked out for me."

"Have you met the male in question?"

"No. We were supposed to meet tomorrow. But I've heard a lot about him, and none of it good."

"Then how do you know how he smells?"

"Because most people smell."

"A fair point. Although you don't."

I sniffed loudly. "I should hope not. I'm a water witch. We bathe at least once a day."

"I approve."

"We also brush our teeth and groom our hair."

"You sound more like a cat than a human."

"Thank you. I think."

"This male water witch must also bathe, then."

"I'm still not interested."

"Maybe he can be encouraged to bathe more regularly to lower the overall stench level."

"I thought you wanted to escape?"

"So did I, but having to chase rats isn't my idea of an escape."

A door squealed open. I pressed my back against the wall of the nearest building. No one exited any of the houses lining the street, and the door slammed shut inexplicably.

"I don't know exactly what he's like. But I've certainly heard enough from people who do know him. Besides, I want to choose my own husband. Is that so difficult to understand?"

Pooky huffed. "That sounds like a lot of hassle. Who cares what he's like? The only question you need to answer is if he can keep me… I mean *us*… in the lifestyle to which we are accustomed. Beyond that, it makes little difference."

"Maybe not to you."

"Exactly my point. Do you see cats complaining when they mate with complete strangers? Of course not! Cats are detached from such matters. Humans and witches could learn a lot from us, if you'd only elevate your minds."

"Are you always this obnoxious?"

"I can't imagine to whom you are addressing that comment. But I'm insulted on his or her behalf."

"You do that. Can you hear anything?"

"Humph. The only thing I hear is your nattering, and my grumbly stomach. It's been at least three hours since I last ate." He clawed up my chest and forced me to stare into his yellow eyes. "Do you know what happens when a cat goes for too long without sustenance? It's dreadful, absolutely dreadful. And I'm a refined cat, requiring refined sustenance on a frequent basis. So look into my eyes, and hear me well. Find me milk."

"You'll have to wait. Now, stop distracting me." I opened my bag, dropped the cat in it and closed it most of the way.

"I swear on my whiskers you'll live to regret that!"

21

"Be careful, cat. I may not be as powerful as Grand Dame Puddlewick, but I know a few good spells and curses. Hush. I think I hear something."

The cat grumbled to himself but must've realized it was more comfortable lying on soft clothing than being jostled in my arms. A moment later, a soft snoring sound drifted out of the bag. But it wasn't loud enough to disguise the *clip clop* of hooves cantering down cobblestoned streets. The horse was coming from the direction of my home. Coincidence? Or my grandmother?

Either way, I was in trouble. If it was a mounted police officer, he'd object to me lurking in the shadows of a respectable home and arrest me on suspicion of criminal intent. And if it was my grandmother...

I hoped it was the police.

I held my breath, silently praying to the gods of runaway brides that the horse would turn at some intersection and gallop off in another direction.

The gods were still sleeping, because the horse was definitely moving in my direction. The echoes of its hooves grew louder, competing with my pounding heart.

Grand Dame Puddlewick was minutes away from finding me. I'd definitely been cursed.

I started to run.

Chapter Three

MY BAG BOUNCED against my side. The pounding of my shoes against cobblestones kept time with my rapid heartbeat. Pooky hissed at every bump, promising to do unsavory things to my clothing. I didn't care. Or rather, I cared but not enough to slow down.

The only thing that mattered now was escaping whoever was coming on horseback. And the more I raced through the night, the more certain I was about the horse rider's identity. It was Grand Dame Puddlewick. Who else had any reason to follow me with such persistence?

Her accursed bolt must've hit me square on my heel.

There was no other explanation. What else but the blue bolt curse could allow her to follow me so accurately? It guided her horse as it maneuvered the streets with unerring precision, always heading in my direction no matter how many turns I took.

"And then do you know what I'm going to do, young witch?" Pooky yowled. "I'm going to cough up *another* hairball. Then another. And just when you think I can't possibly produce another one, guess what? I shall! Your clothes'll be smothered in hairballs by the time I'm done in here."

I didn't bother replying. Hairballs were barely an inconvenience compared to my fate if Grand Dame Puddlewick caught me.

"After the tsunami of hairballs, I'm going to find the biggest, ugliest rat... Come to think of it, they're all ugly. Humph. Well, I'll find the most *flea-infested*, bubonic plague carrying, ugliest rat ever and put it in your bed. That's what I'll do. I'll do it one night when you've forgotten all about this incident. But I shall never forget!"

"Good for you," I huffed, trying to ignore the stitch in my side. "I'll have you know a rat won't disturb me. Grand Dame Puddlewick ensured I had intensive and extensive lessons in anatomy. The tutor required me to handle a fair number of rats with my bare hands during dissections."

"How morbidly fascinating. Did you ever dissect a human cadaver?"

"No, but not from want of trying. Sadly, any available cadaver was immediately snapped up by medical students and researchers. It was one of my grandmother's greatest disappointments. Please stop talking. I'm having trouble breathing."

I needed to work on my fitness level. Grand Dame Puddlewick never approved of any exercise beyond a gentle stroll around the garden. Something about ladylike behavior befitting our station in the Wavily Witch Clan, the need to avoid unseemly conduct, and so on.

I ducked down an alleyway, trying to remember the map of London I'd studied in Father's room. I had a vague sense of where the port was. If nothing else, I could simply follow the foulest smell possible, and it would eventually lead me to the right place.

"I think I bruised my tail tip," Pooky mewed. "You're a brute. A brute in a witch's form. But a brute nonetheless."

I patted the side of my bag with more force than necessary, and lengthened my stride. The stench of raw sewage and unbathed bodies definitely intensified as I ran downhill. I was getting close. But so was the horse. The horse being ridden by my vengeful, meddlesome, marriage-arranging, politically driven grandmother.

"Need… to change… my plan," I gasped as the port came into view.

"You most certainly do," Pooky grumped. "Your plan must allow me to travel in a dignified fashion, one more appropriate for a creature of my rank and station. I say, is this egg edible? I don't normally eat eggs, but desperate times—"

"Don't… touch it."

"Humph. You're in a foul mood."

I'd booked passage on the SS *Cedric* departing on the morning tide, a couple hours after sunrise. That was still several hours away, which meant Grand Dame Puddlewick had plenty of time to explore every passenger ship currently docked in London's harbor. She could easily track my whereabouts by perusing the ships' passenger manifestoes.

Normally manifestoes were private documents, not for public scrutiny. But she wasn't above placing a small token of appreciation in the hands of every single captain in order to find my name and — by extension — me. My plan of escaping to the New World was in grave danger of failing.

I was in a pickle, and only three options came to mind.

Option one: fake my death. A perfectly respectable plan, albeit one requiring me to make a sufficient mess in order to convince everyone of my unfortunate but convenient demise. However, a well-executed fake death required time I didn't have. I also wasn't a fan of mess, either.

Option two: learn a shapeshifting spell. This was more difficult than it sounded. Such a complex spell required years of practice and a few mishaps to perfect. I didn't have years. I hardly had minutes in which to avoid Grand Dame Puddlewick and her curse-guided horse.

Option three: stow away on any ship that *wasn't* the SS *Cedric*, preferably one leaving immediately. That way, my name wouldn't appear in any manifesto.

I loved the idea of a fake death, and positively drooled over learning a powerful spell. Option three was by far the most boring and human. Therefore Grand Dame Puddlewick would never think of it, making it perfect.

"Are you sure I can't eat it?" Pooky asked. "It looks delicious. Soft-boiled—"

"No, you can't. It's my future familiar." The stitch in my side had become a body-devouring spasm. I wrapped my arms around my waist in an effort to hold my lungs in place and staggered onward.

"What sort of familiar?"

"A chicken, I believe. Grand Dame Puddlewick gave me the egg as an engagement present."

"A chicken?" Pooky paused. "That's rather undignified, even for you."

He wasn't wrong. I was both shocked and mortified when Grand Dame Puddlewick presented her gift to me a couple of days ago.

"I've administered every seeker spell I know of," she'd stated, seeker spells being one of her specialities. "The results are unanimous. In this egg is your future familiar. It's about time you had one, considering you're about to join the ranks of the married. Congratulations."

I'd stared at the large egg in the small wicker box and wondered what I'd done to deserve this. Maybe it was her idea of a joke. It wasn't funny. I was grateful we were alone when she'd presented it to me. The public humiliation would've destroyed me.

Pooky sniffed. "It smells funny."

"It does not."

"What if I accidentally ate it? No one will blame you."

"Leave it alone." I ducked into the doorway of a building.

We were now one block away from the port. The upper-class housing of my neighborhood had long since deteriorated into part shantytown, part warehouse district. I was no longer worried about a police officer finding me. I'd be lucky if that happened. I was most definitely in the wrong place at the wrong time.

The *clip clop* of hooves cracked loudly toward me. I crouched in the shadows of a doorway. A horse cantered into view, veering toward the port. A familiar figure sat upon it. The back was rigid and straight. The shoulders, stiff. Her nose imperiously sniffed the air.

"I still think you can do better," Pooky said. "I'd make a brilliant familiar, if I do say so myself. Not that I'm offering."

Grand Dame Puddlewick disappeared around the corner of a large warehouse, no doubt setting her sights on the various passenger ships docked around the public piers. She'd start searching the ones scheduled to sail the soonest. Once she discovered my name, she'd no doubt lurk around the SS *Cedric* until I made my appearance.

My shoulders sagged. I'd avoided detection, but for how long? I was doomed to discovery without the open ocean disrupting her curse or any seeker spells she might use.

I rummaged in my pocket and pulled out a vial of freshwater.

"What're you doing?"

"I'm going to use a seeker spell to find us a safe place to hide. At least, I'll try."

"You'll try?"

"It's a difficult spell. Grand Dame Puddlewick makes it look easy, but it really isn't."

"Get on with it, then."

I tried, but my hands shook. Fear of capture drove the words straight out of my head. "It's no use. I can't."

"Well, this has been fun. I'm sure my human'll be delighted to have me back home. She probably doesn't know I've gone. She has a wretchedly limited imagination."

"I have to keep moving."

"Yes, you do. Wait. You're moving in the *opposite* direction of home."

"I'm not giving up yet."

"I see. An overachiever, are you? How exhausting."

I headed away from the SS *Cedric* and the other passenger ships, toward an older, less utilized and dimly lit section of the port. The buildings became smaller and dingier. Even the air had a derelict quality to it.

"It smells appalling," Pooky muttered. "Where're you taking me?"

"Feel free to walk."

"In this filth?"

"Shh. I see someone." I ducked behind a stack of crates, trying not to breathe too deeply. Pooky was right about the smell. For how long had the products in the crates been dead?

Shadowy figures flitted around a handcart overloaded with barrels. Furtive whispers trickled toward me.

"This it?"

"What the cap'n ordered."

"Hope ol' Tricky knows what's what."

"Dare you to call the ol' cap *old*."

"I'm crazy. I ain't stupid."

The two men laughed softly, a cheerful sound in a dreary location.

"Best get this to the ship right fast. We're sailin' 'fore first light."

"Pity. Was kinda lookin' forward to a day in the big city."

The first man snorted. "You mean the brothels. Tricky don't approve, you know. Hurry up, man. 'Fore the guard wakes up. Cap'n wants to leave right away."

I smiled. I'd found my new ride out of this dilemma. With any luck, I'd slip off at the next port and catch another ship to the New World.

Two bulky men began pulling the handcart. The barrels were heavy, judging by the men's grunts and friendly grumbles. The path began to incline slightly down-hill, and the handcart picked up speed. The men started to jog.

I needed to hurry if I was going to catch my ride. I didn't dare use any magic, not with Grand Dame Puddlewick so close. She was sniffing like a bloodhound for any trace of my magic. I would have to play human until I was well away from English shores. I shuddered at the thought. How did humans manage without magic? I was about to find out.

"Keep quiet," I whispered to my bag and hurried after the cart. It was open at the back, the barrels tied against the sides and each other by thick rope. I grabbed onto the ledge, kicked off and slumped onto the floor of the cart.

"Heard something?" one of the men grunted.

"Your foul breath."

"You can't hear breath."

"Can, too. 'Cause I just did. Yours."

The two men continued arguing the way only best friends can as they guided the cart onto an unlit pier. I slid off and ducked behind a wooden pillar, searching the shadows for sign of a ship. Clouds obscured the stars, and the only light was from a few storm lanterns. It was enough to make out the darker shadow lurking at the end of the pier. A sailing ship.

Gruff voices greeted the two men. A small swarm of sailors gathered around the cart. In short order, the barrels disappeared onto the ship.

My bag sprouted a cat's head as Pooky wiggled halfway out. "We aren't seriously traveling on *that*, are we?"

"Do you see any other mode of transport? A flying carpet, perhaps?"

"I'll take the carpet."

"There's no such thing, Pooky."

"Humph. That over there? It's not transport. It's a drowning accident waiting to happen. You're better off stuffing yourself into one of those barrels and rolling yourself off the pier."

"After you."

"This is a terrible plan. You need a new one."

"I like the old one." I squinted, desperately wishing I spent more time practicing my night vision spell. Instead, I'd become an expert at lock picking, but lock picking wasn't going to put an ocean between me and Grand Dame Puddlewick. "We have no other choice."

"Rubbish. We have many choices. We can abandon this futile plan, go home, and drink some warm cream. No? Then we can catch a coach to Kilkenny. I'm leaning toward the first option. Let's call it a day. I put up with the female human. You marry the toad your grandmother selected for you. Who knows? Maybe he'll turn into a prince if you kiss him."

"You realize that only happens in fairytales."

"It's worth a shot."

"You kiss him, then."

"That will never work."

The sailors retreated onto the ship. It was a decent-sized vessel but by no means as big as the transatlantic ships. It definitely had a fast look to it, though. Probably a merchant who specialized in perishable products like oranges or — gods forbid — slaves. I wasn't keen on joining a band of slave traders if that's what they were.

"On the count of three," I whispered.

"And then what? Do you actually expect me to do anything?"

"Tell me if you see any sailors in my way."

"I can't watch."

Keeping low, I dashed down the pier, pausing behind crates and refuse deposited at random points on the rickety wooden surface. So far, no one had raised an alarm or shouted, "Oi, runaway bride! What're you doing in this part of town at this time of night?"

Two sailors pulled at the plank connecting the ship to the pier. Other men scuttled across the deck, preparing to leave shore.

"Have you reached three yet?" Pooky asked.

"We passed it ten seconds ago," I huffed, searching for another way onto the ship. A large sail flapped in a damp breeze as the sailors released various ropes, tightened others. I couldn't say what they were doing as I'd never sailed in my life.

"I could've sworn we were only on one," Pooky said. "You certainly counted to three very fast. Then again, I've never been big on numbers. It's a human preoccupation. What does it matter if you have three kittens or four? Mama loved us all equally. Except me, of course. She loved me the most."

A heavy chain connected the ship to the ocean bottom. The chain began to tremble, and a metallic squeal made my teeth grit. A few sailors were hauling the anchor up.

"Get ready," I said.

"Again? How many times must I ready myself, and for what? You truly are a mystery."

"You might want to get inside the bag."

"I'm already in the bag."

"I mean entirely inside."

"Why? Is it starting to rain?"

"Actually, yes."

"Abominable weather."

"Don't tell me I didn't warn you. We're going to jump."

"We're doing *what*?"

The salt-scented breeze flung a light drizzle at me, coating my face and clothes with a cool dampness. The wooden planks became slick as I ran toward the chain.

"Here goes," I warned.

"What goes... No, you're not going to... Stop!" Pooky punctuated his sentence with a high-pitched screech as I leaped off the pier, reaching desperately for the anchor chain.

It wasn't a very far jump. But I still gasped with relief when cold, slimy metal scratched at my face.

"You're the worst planner ever," Pooky whispered. "The very worst. And I know about bad planning. My cousin Neville tried to steal a jar of cream from a dairy farm that was guarded by a pack of dogs. I don't have to tell you what happened to Neville, do I? Because I will. In great, gory detail. He decided to…"

I stopped listening and focused on crawling up the chain to a small ledge. It was a good thing I was wearing pantaloons rather than a dress. I couldn't imagine doing any of these theatrics while wearing appropriate feminine attire. Boys certainly had it easy when it came to clothes.

I reached the ledge and pressed myself up against the wooden side of the ship. I had no idea about sailing, but I was pretty sure that once the anchor was secured, we'd head for open waters. And gripping onto the side of a rapidly moving ship wasn't a great option, even for a water witch wearing pantaloons.

I began to inch around the back of the ship, searching for a way in that wouldn't involve me climbing onto the deck. The sailors were busy but not that busy. They'd toss me overboard if they didn't hand me over to the authorities.

"We're hanging over water," Pooky whimpered. "Are you aware of this?"

"Obviously."

"I'm just checking. You know you're certifiably insane?"

"I suppose you have a cousin who's insane, so you know all about this topic as well?"

"An uncle, actually."

"Your family tree doesn't sound too healthy."

"We don't live in a tree, you nincompoop. Trees are for squirrels and birds. Feathery pillows are for cats. I'm going to need a lot of time to educate you on the realities of life."

"How fortunate for me. Here we are."

A sturdy stick propped open a wooden hatch. The opening wasn't particularly big, but more than enough to accommodate my bag, then me. I wiggled through and collapsed, my backside again saved from any indignities by my bag.

"Get... off... Can't... breathe."

I slid down, brushing my hands free of slime and whatever foul debris the chain picked up. "That wasn't too difficult, now was it?"

"Maybe *you* are the one who belongs in a tree with the rest of the squirrels and nuts."

I was still smiling when I looked up and stared down the barrel of a cannon.

Chapter Four

"How CIVILIZED," Pooky purred and scrambled into the mouth of the cannon. "They must worship cats on this ship. A cubbyhole perfectly sized for me. Although they neglected to line it with blankets and a few pillows. Make sure you inform them of this oversight. Nonetheless, it's a decent attempt for a boat of humans."

He sat inside, his tail dangling out of the muzzle, and stared down the cannon's length.

"That's not a cat bed, Pooky."

"There's no need to be jealous. I'm sure they'll find you a suitable location. Perhaps that box over there. All it needs is a blanket, and it'll look just like a bed and almost as cozy."

I reached into my bag, lit a match, and studied the box. More specifically, the warning signs on the box. "That's also *not* a bed. It contains cannon balls."

"Delightful. Truly delightful."

I stood up, staring around the space in which we found ourselves. Several barrels — most likely the ones on the

VERED EHSANI

cart I'd followed — lined one wall. Their labels declared the contents as gunpowder.

Two other cannons squatted in the rectangular room. All three had their own window in the ship's hull. Windows through which the cannons could be used to shoot at another ship.

"What sort of merchant ship requires three cannons?"

"The one sailing through dangerous waters, I imagine." Pooky began grooming himself. "We have to work on your imagination."

"Do go on."

"Maybe the ship sails through pirate-infested waters, for example. Fighting pirates justifies at least three cannons."

"I suppose."

"To be clearer, water is *always* dangerous. I don't understand why any creature in its right or wrong mind would venture forth willingly into it. Yet humans do it all the time, which is proof how terribly wrong their minds are. It's nothing short of miraculous they've lasted as long as they have. They never should've climbed down from the trees. Are you listening to me?"

I touched the wick jutting out from the back of one cannon. Fine soot coated my fingers. "This has been used recently."

"They've been sailing through dangerous waters recently. Do keep up with the conversation. Aren't you the one who wants to sail off the edge of the Old World and drop onto the new one? Well, ships which do that have to have cannons."

"Perhaps you're right."

"Perhaps... *Perhaps?*" Pooky spluttered. "There's no *perhaps* about it. My ancestor Sir Dedrick Bartholomew Pocock O'Doherty the First accurately predicted—"

The ship lurched. Pooky hissed, his back arching. I staggered against the cold, dark metal of the closest cannon. Male voices shouted from above, canvas snapped in the breeze, and waves sloshed against the hull.

We were sailing away from shore.

My smile returned, and I spun in a circle with my arms stretched out. I'd done it. I'd successfully escaped Grand Dame Puddlewick and her machinations. No longer was I a pawn in her power play within the Wavily Clan. I was free. Free to dream. Free to imagine a new life. So what if I required lessons from a cat in these matters? I was finally—

"Who the blasted barnacles are ye?"

A heavyset man stood at the entrance of the armory, storm lantern in one hand, sword in the other, and a fierce glare directed straight at me. He took a step closer. Wood knocked against wood. He had a peg leg.

"Oh, look. It's a man servant. Finally. I'm about to lose a life if I don't eat soon." Pooky dropped off the cannon, landing with a heavy *thunk*, and waddled toward the sailor. "You with the tree leg. I require a dish of cream instantly. Milk, if you don't have any cream. While you're here, your finest linen, at least one feather-filled pillow and a soft blanket wouldn't go amiss, either. Are you listening to me? Humph. Of course not. You're human." He looked back at me. "Translate."

The sailor stared at Pooky, his frown twitching into a reluctant smile. "Ain't ye a beauty?"

Pooky purred. "You hear that? He thinks I'm beautiful. He's correct, of course. Please translate my request to him. It's a good thing I have you along to communicate on my behalf."

The sailor stooped, set down the lantern, and plucked Pooky up by the scruff of his neck. The cat hissed and howled, pawing at the man's chest. But the sailor held him too far out for the claws to do any damage. "We need us a rat catcher."

"A rat *what*? Did he say a… *cough, cough*… a rat catcher? I hope he's referring to you."

"Probably not," I said.

"Leave this to me," Pooky said. "I'm a master at hypnosis. Human, look into my eyes. Deeper… *Deeper*. You are now under my command."

"Yer cat's creepy. An' fat," the one-legged sailor muttered.

"I'm *not* fat. My fur's *fluffy*! Tell him."

The sailor lifted his sword and waggled it at me. "As fer ye. Down the hall, and up those stairs. Right now." He stepped aside and indicated to a set of stairs at the end of a narrow, dimly lit corridor.

"Tell this ruffian to unhand me at once. Such a lack of respect. What does he think I am, a dog?"

"Sorry, Pooky," I murmured, trying to stand straight even though my legs wobbled. I took a deep breath, then forced myself to walk past the angry sailor.

"Up!" the sailor ordered when I reached the narrow, steep, rickety stairs.

The peg leg stomped behind me, an echo of my heart-beat. How was the man managing the stairs? I was clinging onto both handrails and still struggling. He was carrying a howling cat and a sword. Maybe he'd put his sword away. I was tempted to check, but what then? He could easily drop the cat and pull out his sword before I had time to summon a spell.

A light rain pelted against the deck, but it didn't slow down the hectic activity. Sailors ran back and forth, climbing up masts, running along booms, climbing down ladders, and doing other sailor things.

"Cap'n, found us a stowaway, I did."

The blur of activity slowed down, pausing briefly as every sailor stared at me. Expressions ranged from curiosity to outright hostility, with one or two wincing in sympathy.

"Thank the cat goddess. They're summoning their leader," Pooky yelped. "You make sure to tell them I'm royalty, descendent from the Egyptian goddess—"

"Not now," I whispered.

"A stowaway, eh?"

I gawked as a middle-aged woman stomped onto the deck. "You're the…? But you're a—"

"Captain. I believe that's the word you're looking for. I'm the captain of this here fine vessel." The captain looked over my shoulder, a black pipe clenched in her teeth. "Where'd you find the lad, Stubbs?"

"Pilferin' our arms, Cap'n Tricky, he was."

"I was not," I protested.

One of the other sailors stepped close to the captain, a wide grin on his darkly tanned face. "Don't think he's a lad, Tricky."

Tricky puffed, exhaling a ring of smoke. "I believe you're correct, Quill."

"How dare you," I said, then noticed the man's attention on my chest. I glanced down.

The light rain and ocean mist had pressed a film of water against my shirt. It was obvious I had a couple of items a boy normally wouldn't. Scowling, I pulled my jacket tightly around me and buttoned it up.

Some of the sailors hooted, whistled or cheered.

The captain held up her fist. Silence returned, but the men continued gawking at me, as if they'd never seen a young woman dressed in pantaloons. They allowed a woman to be captain but found me odd?

"Don't you useless lot have better things to do?" the captain barked.

Men scuttled away, quickly finding something else to do. Despite the captain's threatening glare, a few chose activities conveniently close enough to observe what fate the captain had in store for me.

Quill remained by the captain's side, still beaming like he'd discovered the cure for cholera. I wished he would, since at least he'd be doing something useful.

The captain straightened her shoulders and strutted toward me. "Well, let's hear it, then."

"My name," Pooky hissed. "Tell them my name. Sir Dedrick. Bartholomew. Pocock. O'Doherty the Third. Descended from royalty and the cat goddess—"

"This is Pooky," I said, indicating the cat still in Stubbs' grip.

"That's not my name!"

Tricky glanced at Pooky. "It certainly makes a lot of noise."

"Yes, it does," I said. "I sometimes imagine it's talking to me."

"I *am* talking to you! Save me. Please, save me!" Pooky whined pitifully.

The captain's dark eyebrows lifted upward. She sucked on her pipe, then removed it. "Enough about the feline. Who're you?"

"I'm Miss Storm…" My teeth clicked together sharply, biting back my last name.

These were definitely humans, so I had to take care not to reveal my true nature to them. They might decide to hand me over to the authorities for a good flogging or burning.

More importantly, Grand Dame Puddlewick was known among regular people as a wealthy businesswoman. If I told them my full name…

People — humans and witches alike — talked. It would

be my luck for the wrong people to talk to the wrong people, and for word to reach Grand Dame Puddlewick. She had a vast network of informants, so it wasn't beyond the realm of possibility.

"Miss Storm *what*?"

I forced a smile. "Nothing else. Just Miss Storm."

Tricky's teeth clicked on her pipe's stem. "That it?"

"That's it."

"Miss your first name?"

My smile became brittle. "No. Storm is."

"No family name?"

"None I care to remember."

A couple of the sailors chuckled until the captain twisted her head toward them. They became very busy scrubbing the decks.

"I can pay for my passage," I offered. "Although I have one concern. Do you have tea leaves on your ship?"

The sailor next to the captain — Quill — guffawed. The loud, booming noise made me want to join him, even though I had no reason to laugh or even smile at this point. "Oi! She's worried 'bout tea leaves, mateys!"

Stubbs pressed a finger into my back. "Blasted barnacles. Ain't no passenger ship, this ain't, missy."

The captain chomped on the tip of her pipe, a faint upturn of her mouth suggesting a smile. She didn't have a lot of smiling lines, so I suspected this was a rare occasion. "Stubbs is correct." Her gaze intentionally drifted upward, to the top of the tallest mast.

I followed the direction of her gaze and gasped. A Jolly Roger flapped forlornly in the damp breeze. So you're..." I gulped. "Pirates?"

The entire crew shouted, "Hurrah!"

"Oh. Well, I... I mean, that's... Is that a... a pink flag?"

"Why, yes. Yes, it is. Where are my manners?" The captain performed a mock bow. "I'm Olivia Twitchett Trickett, Captain of *The Pink Pearl*. And this handsome gentleman is Shaun Quill, my quartermaster."

"Pink—" I stuttered.

"So you see, Miss Storm or whoever you really are, you most certainly chose the wrong ship."

Quill winked. "'Tis fate, it is. You'll be a pirate."

"What a scandalous idea!" I cried. "I've no intention of engaging in the pirating profession."

"Why not?"

"For a start, sir, I don't approve of your lifestyle."

"Our lifestyle's fantastic. Ain't that so, mateys?"

"Hurrah!"

"And we're the nice kind of pirates," Quill added.

"There're no such pirates."

"Aye, there is. We steal from the rich to give to the poor."

"To which poor do you give?"

"Us, o' course. We're from the poor class."

"So you're offering me a life of robbing and pillaging."

"Don't forget romance an' adventure."

"Hurrah!"

"I'll have to decline," I said. "Blood stains are notoriously difficult to remove from clothing."

"We don't maim nor murder no one. It's not our way."

"Enough," Tricky said. "Seems she's not interested, which makes her a stowaway."

"Useless stowaways walk the plank, they do," Stubbs growled and paused while the crew provided another loud *Hurrah*. "Ain't that right? Walk the plank."

"Walk the plank!" several pirates shouted with unseemly enthusiasm.

"This is the pirate way," Quill said, rubbing the stubble

on his cheeks. "Unless they're particularly pretty." He studied me, perhaps trying to figure out if I qualified for plank walking or some other dastardly fate.

"I bet you wish you'd married your grandmother's toad now," Pooky said.

"Blasted barnacles," Stubbs grumbled. "Maybe she be a witch. Black cat an' all."

"I…" I gawked at him. How would a human react? "How rude!"

"She's also pretty, she is," Stubbs added. "The chief, then?"

Quill nodded. "Definitely. That okay with you, Tricky?"

Tricky looked heavenwards. "I suppose, unless she proves herself useful. But the decision'll have to wait until after the pirate parlay."

"What does that all mean?" I demanded.

"It means they only consider you *pretty*," Pooky purred. "Did you hear what the tree-legged one called me? Beautiful."

"Chief Ali Babak's always lookin' to add to his harem," Stubbs said.

"His harem!"

"Aye."

"And we can trade you for some o' that camel milk o' his," Quill added. "That'd be a nice change."

I folded my arms and glared at the pirates. "I went through great effort to escape one arranged marriage. I most certainly have no intention of entering another."

"Don't fuss, Miss Storm," Quill said. "He's a nice enough chap. You don't have to marry if you don't want. He's got enough wives, anyway. He'll just add you to his collection o' concubines, that's all."

"His…" I gulped.

"Although he's got a lot o' them as well. So maybe he'll marry you, after all. That'll make you the one hundredth and one woman in his household. Sounds like a lucky number."

"One hundred and one!"

"Aye." Quill winked at me. "Unless you prove useful. Then we'll keep you."

"An' the cat can earn its keep by catchin' us some blasted rats. Ain't that right, wee kitty?" Stubbs shook Pooky.

"Told you we should've gone to Kilkenny," Pooky muttered.

Chapter Five

THE PIRATES cheerfully agreed on their intention to trade me for camel milk. They then left me to my own devices. Tricky gave me a warning look, then marched back to her cabin.

"That female scares me," Pooky whispered.

I gulped. "Me, too."

Stubbs offered to make me a bed in the pantry. He threatened me the entire time if I dared steal so much as a grain of sugar or a pinch of snuff.

"I don't indulge in snuff, and I prefer my tea pure," I finally informed him.

Stubbs shrugged. "Yer blasted loss." He tossed a lumpy, heavily stained mattress onto the floor, added a thin, tattered blanket and what I assumed was meant to be a pillow, then limped away. His wooden leg clicked heavily against the floorboards.

"I hope they're joking about expecting me to catch rats," Pooky said as he lounged next to a small tin of precious sugar.

"We have bigger problems than that, Pooky." I started pacing the long, narrow pantry.

"We certainly do. I don't see or smell a hint of cream. How do these humans survive? Can I eat your egg?"

"What… No! That's my future familiar, apparently."

Pooky clawed at the small wicker box, then glared balefully at me. "You can buy another chicken later."

"This is the one my grandmother selected for me."

"Who cares? She's not here. I didn't want to have to do this, but you leave me no choice. Look into my eyes. Deeper. You are now under my command. Feed me!"

I stepped away from the cat. "What are you doing?"

"Hypnotizing you, of course. It's my secret power."

"It's not working."

"Of course it is. You're already reaching for the egg."

"To remove it from under your paw."

"Why do you need a familiar, anyway?"

"To help me with my spells. My magic is a bit…"

"Bad?"

"*Unfocused.* And slow. Having my own familiar will help me focus my spells better and speed up my reaction time."

"You mean I'm stuck with a dunce witch?"

"No. I merely require a bit of assistance now and then." I flinched. Those were the exact words Grand Dame Puddlewick had used, but her tone wasn't as kind. I shook my head to clear the memory. "At any rate, we need to keep a low profile."

"Humph. Let me try this again. Look deeply into my eyes."

"Stop it! They're going to give me to a chief. I'll live out my days as the hundredth and one concubine or wife in a harem. If Grand Dame Puddlewick ever found out, she'd be mortified. And she'd leave me there to punish me for daring to run away."

Pooky stretched luxuriously. "I wonder if they have sardines? That's a reasonable substitute for cream. Not a perfect substitute by any stretch of the imagination, but I can manage. Go ask them if they have any sardines."

I stopped pacing and swatted at the cat. "Go make yourself useful before they use you as fish bait."

The cat lifted one of his front paws. His claws punched out. "They wouldn't dare."

"They're pirates. Daring is part of their lifestyle."

He patted the tin of sugar, knocking it aside.

I lunged and grabbed the tin before it could fall. "Do you want to get us tossed overboard? Sugar is a precious commodity. I'm surprised this one isn't locked away."

"The only commodity worth locking up is—"

"Yes, yes. I'll see what I can find for your breakfast."

I didn't know a cat could smile, but Pooky came close to it. His smug little face squirreled up, and he licked his lips. "And about time. I'm self-digesting over here."

My stomach gurgled in sympathy. I didn't have time to worry about it. The rest of the day was a blur of bumpy waves, salt spray, and visitors. A long, steady stream of pirates found excuses to visit the pantry. They pretended not to see me until they almost stumbled over or into me, then spluttered their apologies, provided their names, inquired after my health, and asked if I needed anything.

Quill was the most gracious and persistent. "Anything you need, let me know. After all, I'm the quartermaster, and that position comes with benefits." He lifted his chin, peered down at me and waited for me to acknowledge his title.

I glanced at Pooky, who shrugged and continued licking his chest. "Congratulations?"

The man deflated slightly. "You don't know what that means, do you? I'm second in command after the captain.

The men listen to me. I'm also in charge o' food and water supplies."

"Food!" Pooky leaped upward. "Ask him about cream. And sardines."

"Are you hungry?" Quill asked, ignoring the cat. "Thirsty?"

"I'd love a cup of tea and toast."

"I can't give you sugar with your tea, but we're otherwise fully stocked."

"Marvelous."

"And cream," Pooky hissed. "Don't forget—"

I indicated the cat. "Do you have anything I can feed him?"

"'Til he starts catchin' rats, you mean?" Quill asked.

"Sure. Until then."

Pooky flopped onto the shelf. "I see I shall have to fend for myself." He heaved himself to the edge. "A little help getting down, if you please. And then I shall wander off in a self-righteous huff. Rats. Humph!"

By the end of the day, I felt confident I had met most if not all of the crew. I was less confident I could manage to cross the vast ocean to the New World. The little bit I'd eaten in the morning didn't stay down long. The pirates chuckled good-naturedly as I leaned over the guardrail and ejected my breakfast into the ocean.

Stubbs grumbled about the uselessness of landlubbers, but he dutifully came by with a cup of tea and added a dose of a suspicious-smelling liquid into it. "It'll settle yer blasted tummy, it will. Lickety-split."

Scotty the sailing master called it, "Buildin' your sea legs, lassie."

I called it a waste of half-decent food.

The cooks, Khalif and Khalid, became my best friends. The Persian twins managed to find the one item I could consume without immediately rushing to the guardrail: ginger. Ginger tea. Candied ginger. Raw ginger. I was sweating ginger through my pores.

We sailed for three days. We were going south, and the weather became progressively warmer. By the time we reached our destination, I was no longer wearing a jacket, nor was I spending every waking minute leaning over the rails, wishing I hadn't eaten anything.

As the sun set, a small island appeared in the horizon. The pirates gathered along one side of the deck, chatting excitedly. I was relieved we'd found land, and prayed the chief wasn't there.

"We've arrived, Miss Storm," Monks shouted at me over the hubbub.

I nodded at the boy. He was at most twelve years old. As the powder monkey, he assisted the gun crew in prepping the cannons during battle. I hoped to never see him at his official job. He spent most of the time swabbing the main deck and running errands.

Captain Tricky stood on the forecastle at the front of the ship, fists on her waist as she surveyed the island. "We made good time, lads. Behold. Treasure Island."

"Hurrah!" the crew shouted.

"Let's hear what the pirate king has to say at this parlay," she added.

"Aye. And pray the food's better this year than last," McCormick the master gunner said, earning a few cheers.

"Remember, fellow buccaneers." Tricky held up a large, leather-bound book. "Remember your oath in the Codex of *The Pink Pearl*. This is the pirate way."

"This is the pirate way," others murmured.

I turned to Monks. "What's that book?"

"It's our code," he enthused. "We all sign our mark when we join. It tells what's what. Like reward, punishment, division o' loot. All the ships have one. The king has the biggest."

"King!" Pooky clawed his way to the top of the rail. "Here's the plan, witch. You grovel before him and beg for mercy. Explain to him that your cat is royalty, just like he is, and can't be expected to chase after vermin. Who knows? The king might take pity on you, too, and allow you to join me in royal comfort."

I patted Pooky on the head, being careful to knock him onto the deck rather than into the ocean.

"And if not," Pooky screeched, "I shall stay here with Khalid or Khalif or whatever their names are. At least the cooks know how to treat a cat."

Several other pirate ships were already anchored in the natural harbor on one side of the island. Cheers and jeers echoed across the water as the different crews greeted each other.

Tricky joined the rest of *The Pink Pearl's* crew on the main deck, surveying the scene. The book was no longer in her hand.

"Why here?" I asked.

"It's the pirate way," Tricky intoned.

"It's the pirate way," echoed her crew.

"Hmm. But that isn't actually an explanation."

"It'll have to do. Come along, Miss Storm," Tricky ordered as she clambered down a ladder and leaped into a rowboat.

I peered over the guardrail. "Isn't there a pier we can use?"

Scotty chuckled. He was a small man with a thick mop of black hair and a quick laugh. He was also the sailing master, a position of great respect. According to Quill, the position required a level of education that was beyond the average sailor or pirate. "No, lass. This here's no man's land. Because no man — or beggin' your pardon, no woman — has claim on it. So no pier, no nothin' but sand and jungle. In the boat we go."

I climbed down the ladder, wincing as the blisters on my hands from climbing the anchor chain scratched against the rope.

"Don't leave me," Pooky wailed and leaped onto my head.

His weight unbalanced me, and I tilted backward. My hands were sweaty from the exertion of climbing down the ladder. They slipped. My arms windmilled in a desperate attempt to defy gravity. I failed and began to fall.

Chapter Six

POOKY YOWLED, his claws digging into my scalp. I had a moment to regret my inability to perform spells in a speedy fashion. I then added to the list of regrets my decision to hide in a pirate ship. And why didn't I go to Kilkenny?

I then plummeted into Quill's arms.

He gripped me tightly against his broad chest, staring down at me with a cheeky grin. I wanted to protest but was too flustered to speak. Since he'd saved me from landing in the water, I whispered, "Thank you."

He winked and set me on a bench. "Take care, Miss Storm. I might not always be here to catch you, though I'll do my best."

"I'm sure," I muttered.

Pooky mewed, slipping off my head. "What about me!"

I snagged the cat and set him on my lap.

Tricky blew smoke out of her nose, giving me a once-over. "Try not to fall in. Not many here can swim out to save you. Right, then, men. Row hard. They're about to light the bonfire. Move!"

As if on cue, the other ships started disgorging rowboats. A swarm of the small vessels floated across the water, men heaving on the oars. The beach was crowded with pirates by the time we landed.

"You're lucky," Scotty said and smiled broadly. "This here's for pirate folk only. Never heard of no non-pirate comin' to the pirate parlay, at least none that lived to tell the tale." He laughed uproariously, and Quill joined him.

"Delightful," I said.

Scotty wiped tears of mirth away. "Are you a bettin' type, lass?"

"Absolutely not."

"Very wise but not very interestin'."

"Poppycock! Betting is a dreadful vice."

"But a fun one."

"Never you mind, Miss Storm," Quill said as we strolled up the sandy beach toward the large pile of wood stacked for the bonfire. "Scotty here makes bets on everythin' possible."

"That I do. We even had a wager on how long 'fore you'd stop chuckin' the twins' good food overboard." He chuckled, his eyes twinkling. "I won fair and square. Didn't I, Quill?"

Quill smirked. "Not sure 'bout the *fair* part, but you did square away some coin. Mostly at Stubbs' expense."

"Aye, I did. And I'll be squarin' away more 'fore these three days are done. Sure I can't tempt you, Miss Storm? There's a good chance to win or lose some gold on the kingly elections."

"No, thank you. It hardly matters to me who wins."

"You may be right." Scotty paused. "But if you do want to place a wager, the current pirate king is the favored candidate, followed by Captain Rodney."

"Fabulous. How many of these events are there?"

"A pirate parlay? This here's the sixty-second session, you know."

"Is it an annual event, then?"

Quill nodded, pushing between Scotty and me. "It is. And votin' for the pirate king is an annual tradition, as well. It's an elected position, you see."

"So I gathered."

"An honorary position, more like. Though he does earn a bit from the tribute paid to him at the end o' the parlay. The votin' always attracts a few candidates at least. It's hotly contested."

The men jostled to get closer to the stack of wood, but Quill was larger than most. He cheerfully elbowed pirates aside, clearing a path for Scotty and me. I was grateful for their presence. Tricky had already abandoned me, and I didn't care to imagine what my fate would be if I was left unaccompanied, without a protective escort. While I was still dressed as a boy, I didn't trust my disguise to pass close scrutiny.

We reached the large fire pit. Pooky protested vociferously when I tried to put him down.

"You expect me to sit on *that*?" he argued, glaring at the sand.

I didn't reply as Quill was leaning close to me, giving me the names of the captains and other pirates of interest. The only thing I was interested in was a hasty retreat to *The Pink Pearl* where I could indulge in a cup of Khalid's ginger and green tea.

An older, bowlegged man exited the jungle that edged the beach. He lifted up a trumpet and blew on it. The pirates settled down to a restless silence.

"Make way, make way for the pirate king. Brownbeard the Barbaric is here! So it has been decreed."

I choked on a laugh. "Brownbeard?"

Quill pressed his mouth almost against my ear, which was far too close for my comfort or social standards. "The name Blackbeard was already taken, so he had to settle for the next color. Still, it has a nice ring, no?"

Pooky cowered in my arms, his claws poking out. "He sounds like a nincompoop."

I was grateful no one else could understand the cat. It was bad enough I did.

A tall, well-dressed man strutted onto the beach, followed by an escort appropriate for a king. The man wore a powdered wig topped with a black crown. His clothes were brown, from the shiny leather boots to the soft leather vest he wore over a loose white shirt. He was the epitome of what I imagined a pirate to look like, down to his fierce, bushy beard. He lifted a hand and waved indulgently at his subjects.

"All hail Brownbeard the Barbaric, our pirate king!" the bowlegged man shouted.

A halfhearted "Hail the king" rose up from the crowd.

Brownbeard the Barbaric snapped his fingers. A couple of pirates ran ahead of him with a wooden throne which they placed on a low platform built in front of the fire pit.

The king sat on the throne, repositioned his crown, and held up both arms. "Hear me, oh pirates of the three oceans."

"I thought there were four," I whispered.

"Hush," Scotty said. "The king don't like to be interrupted, lass."

"I hereby open the sixty-second annual pirate parlay."

"Hurrah!"

"We have a busy three days ahead of us, my pirate brethren. Scribbles, my scribe, wishes to remind you there will be a strict cease-fire order in place for the full three days and nights of this party… I mean parlay."

The pirates chuckled appreciatively. A few called out, "Hurrah!"

"This means no fighting, even if the other pirate started it."

"But what if he really, *really* started it, your Royal Barbarian?" someone shouted from the back of the crowd.

"You still *really* can't fight him, Sharkbite," the king insisted. "No dueling. No maiming—"

"Not even a wee bit?" a pirate near me asked.

"Not even a little, teensy, wee bit. And I'm looking at you, Squidly." The king jabbed a finger at the pirate who'd asked.

Squidly started to tremble. He yanked his sword out of its scabbard, then dropped it, pointy end on his foot. "Ouch."

"As I was saying," the king continued. "No name calling, no fighting, no dueling, no maiming, no bruising, no killing. And definitely no biting 'cause that's just rude."

"What if someone steals our sugar?"

Everyone around me groaned.

"I brought a packet of my personal stash with me to use during the parlay," the man persisted. "And it's gone. Gone, I tell you!"

"That sugar fiend," Scotty muttered.

"What and who?" I asked.

Quill grinned. "Captain Rodney's quartermaster, Sweetie. He's always complainin' 'bout his precious sugar stash being stolen. He's a bit of an addict, you see."

"A bit?" Scotty laughed. "The man can't function without it."

"Aye. He has his own wax and a seal. Uses them to

stamp his packets shut, so he can tell if anyone's broken into his stash or what."

"Heard the same, I did. Wonder who he'll accuse of thievery this year?"

Sweetie raised his voice. "As you know, I'm a generous soul. I always reward whoever returns my items to me. No questions asked."

"Your reward stinks!" someone at the back of the crowd shouted. "No one wants a private tea party with the likes of you."

"If you had a trace of sense in you, you would!" Sweetie yelled above the laughter.

"Yes, yes, Sweetie," the pirate king said, shouting above the hushed conversations. "Any problems, direct it to your captains."

"What if the captain favors the thief?" Sweetie persisted. "Yes, I'm looking at you, Terrence Winks Wimble! Part quartermaster… Bah! No such position exists on any other ship but *The Red-Eyed Squid*."

A cheerful looking fellow held up both hands. "I swear on me sword, I did no such thin', Sweetie. I don't eat sugar. Bad for me allergies, it is."

"You're a liar, Winks! You did it, you sugar thief! And I'll prove it soon enough."

Boos and hisses accompanied Sweetie as he stomped away from the fire pit, shoving other pirates aside.

"If your captains have any problems, they can come directly to me," Brownbeard said. "So no stealing. Add that to the list, Scribbles. Especially no stealing sugar. We don't want a repeat of the fifty-first, now do we?"

Quill and Scotty murmured agreement along with numerous other pirates.

"The fifty-first?" I whispered.

"The fifty-first pirate parlay," Quill whispered back. "Bad news, that one. We don't like to talk about it."

Brownbeard nodded at the bowlegged pirate who pulled out a scroll and wrote something on the end of it. The pirates quieted down, grinning and nodding, pressing in closer.

"And now, the agenda. Scribbles here will leave the full list posted on that tree over yonder, along with the candidates for kingship." The king pointed at his scribe, then at the closest tree.

"Don't forget the bettin' pool," Scotty yelled.

"Hurrah!"

"You're really going to bet on an election?" I whispered as excited chatter drowned out the king's attempt to answer.

Scotty's smile widened. "Course we are! Every year, we wager on who'll win the vote. Brownbeard's been winnin' for as long as he's been captain. And that's years."

"Aye, he's favored to win again this year," Quill added.

"Of course, Scotty," the king answered less enthusiastically than before. "How could I forget the betting pool? It'll be posted on the same tree with the rules."

"What if we can't read?" Quill shouted.

"Then my scribe here will translate for you. Scribbles, read the agenda, then the current list of candidates."

Scribbles nodded, stepped forward and held out the scroll.

"We've got an informative workshop on better ways to pillage. Also a talk about the top five tricks to improve your cannon prepping techniques. Number four will blow your mind but not your ship."

An appreciative murmur stirred among the crowd.

"How to identify and cure scurvy, always an important topic. Not to be underestimated, mateys. There's a cooking class guaranteed to teach ten ways to cook rotten meat so it doesn't taste like maggots. And of course, no pirate parlay is complete without the pirate olympics."

"Hurrah!" the pirates shouted and clapped.

Scribbles waited for the noise to settle. "All participants who survive to the end of the parlay will enjoy a feast hosted by your king, and receive a worthy memento: a hand-crafted leather scabbard, provided for this event by an artisan in exchange for not getting pillaged."

"Hurrah!"

"On to the election. Current candidates for position of pirate king. Please raise your fist when your name is called. His Royal Nastiness Brownbeard the Barbaric."

Claps and cheers interrupted the announcement.

"Captain Rodriguez Montoya."

A heavily scarred, burly pirate stepped to the front of the crowd and held up both fists.

"Go, Wee Rodney!" a woman shouted.

Pirates sniggered.

Captain Rodney went purple in the face. "Ma, not now! You're embarrassing me!"

"Terrence Winks Wimble. And the king's very own quartermaster Pepe Le Pirate—"

"Oi! Small Foot's runnin' fer king," a pirate hooted.

The crowd broke into laughter and applause. Pepe had just reached the front of the crowd and lifted a fist. His expression darkened for a moment before his mouth stretched into a tight smile.

Scotty whispered, "The man's feet are wee, bitty things. 'Bout your size, lass, despite his height. You know what they say 'bout a man's feet."

Tricky made a disapproving noise, and Scotty didn't continue.

"What do they say?" Pooky asked.

I shrugged.

Scribbles waved until he had everyone's attention again. "Any captain or quartermaster who wishes to place his name for consideration must do so by midnight tonight. The pirates shall vote for the one who best demonstrates the qualities of pirate king. Strong leadership. Good crew management. Effective law enforcement. And a fearsome reputation."

"Hurrah!"

Quill leaned toward me. "Reputation is everythin'. The bloodthirstier, the better, even if no blood be spilled."

"If a quartermaster happens to win the crown," Scribbles said, "he—"

"Or she," Quill shouted and nodded at Tricky.

Scribbles harrumphed. "He — or *she* — automatically becomes captain of his ship as well, and his — or *her* — captain takes the role of quartermaster. So it has been decreed."

The pirate king waved imperiously at Scribbles, who set aside his scroll and gestured to a young boy. The boy held out a torch almost as big as he was.

Brownbeard the Barbaric stood. "And with this flame, I shall officially open the sixty-second pirate parlay—"

A piercing scream interrupted the king.

The king frowned and stared over the crowd. "Who dares interrupt His Royal Nastiness with a sound so unbecoming of a pirate?"

"Beggin' your pardon for the unpirately noise, your Barbaric Royalness," a voice said as someone pushed through the crowd.

"What is it, Stinker?" the king asked and pinched the bridge of his nose.

"Thing is, sir, Quartermaster Sweetie—" the man huffed.

"What about him? Has someone already stolen the rest of his precious sugar stash from the ship?"

Several pirates laughed and jeered.

Stinker shook his head. "No, your Barbaric Highness. Some rat gone and murdered him. Quartermaster Samuel Sweetie McFarson... well, sir, he's dead."

Chapter Seven

A MOMENT of silence followed the announcement of Samuel Sweetie McFarson's murder.

The young boy must not have heard the news, for he held up the flaming torch, speared the bonfire and shouted, "Hurrah!"

The bonfire burst into flames, and happy sparks swirled overhead, reaching for the star-cluttered sky.

A spattering of *hurrahs* echoed the boy's call, and he grinned at the otherwise confused crowd.

"How'd ye know he's blasted murdered?" Stubbs asked, scowling at the messenger of bad news.

The man stepped away. "There be a knife in his chest, that's how."

Several pirates nodded and hummed in agreement.

"Maybe he done fell on it by his bad self," Stubbs persisted.

I snorted in disbelief. "Yes, I'm sure that's exactly what he did. He ran back to his tent and promptly fell upon a knife."

The pirates all turned to me, the silence deepening.

"Good job with keeping a low profile," Pooky muttered and retreated deeper into my arms. He tried to tuck his head in my armpit.

"And who be you?" Scribbles asked.

"Good question, Scribbles," Brownbeard said. "Well, lad. Answer."

"He ain't no lad," Quill said. "He's a she."

Appreciative whistles and catcalls filled the beach.

"Shouldn't we focus on the unfortunate demise of quartermaster Sweetie?" I asked.

"Keep talking," Pooky hissed. "Distract them while I sneak away to safety. Or rather, you carry me and run. That's a much better plan."

"Hurrah!" somebody shouted, then gulped as no one echoed the call.

"This here's supposed to be a no-kill zone." Captain Rodney glared over the bonfire at the pirate king. "It be one of your jobs to keep the peace here, or at least avoid war and other inconveniences. Ain't that so, mateys?"

More nodding and murmuring of agreement were followed by another round of "Hurrah!"

"What do you want, Rodney?" the king asked, his tone as weary as his expression. He slumped in his throne.

Rodney puffed out his broad chest. "That's Captain Rodriguez Montoya to you."

Quill nudged me with an elbow. "Sure, but his ma calls him Wee Rodney."

Pirates around us giggled.

As if Quill's words had summoned her, a shrill voice pierced the unhappy rumblings of the pirates. "Rodney, it's almost your bedtime!"

"I'm busy, Ma!" Rodney roared back.

More laughter drifted through the crowd.

"They're not terribly upset that one of their own has

been murdered," I whispered.

Stubbs grunted, but Quill answered. "Quartermaster Sweetie wasn't very popular. There's some that're more than happy to see him gone."

Rodney beat a fist on his chest, then pointed at Brownbeard. "You ain't fit for that throne, Brownbeard."

"That's Captain Brownbeard the Barbaric, the pirate king, to the likes of you," Scribbles yelled.

"Well said, Scribbles. Well said," the king murmured.

A sharply dressed pirate standing next to the king stepped forward. "It seems to me you're the main benefactor of this murder, Captain Rodriguez."

Rodney's huffing was audible in the hush that settled over the pirates. "Watch your tongue, Pepe Le Pirate, or I'll remove it."

"Threatening to break the peace pact again, are you?"

"I didn't—"

Pepe addressed the audience. "I imagine my captain, our king and my dear friend Brownbeard will fall in the ranks after this scandalous event. And who'll benefit most? Why, Captain Rodney. His position will rise, partly due to a sympathy vote."

"I don't need no one's sympathy to win."

"Did I say sympathy? I meant pity."

Rodney roared wordlessly and stepped toward Pepe. Several pirates pulled him back until he'd regained self-control. Pepe smiled as Rodney retreated into the crowd.

Wood crackled loudly, and some of it tumbled, causing flames and more sparks to leap upward temporarily. When the fire had settled down, the pirate king was standing.

"Hear me well, my fellow pirates. Your king speaks. By the end of the three days, I'll find the culprit who broke our peace accord, and deal with him as pirate code requires. I'll march the traitor to the plank and beyond."

"Hurrah!" every pirate shouted, and the fire trembled before their cheer.

"In the meantime, none of you scoundrels is to leave the environs of this here Treasure Island. Everyone stays on the beach or in the harbor. Hear me well."

"Hurrah!"

"There shall be none who'll doubt the strength of this pirate king," Brownbeard concluded and marched away from his throne, his entourage scrambling to keep up as he stalked toward an elaborate tent set up at the far end of the beach.

More rumblings and mumblings as the pirates began to disperse. Some returned to their rowboats while others began setting up camp on the beach.

"What was that all about?" I asked.

"Rodney basically challenged Brownbeard for the throne," Quill supplied. "He's been eyein' that throne since he was big enough to hold a sword. And now's his chance. Whoever murdered Sweetie has presented Captain Rodney with the perfect chance."

"How convenient," I murmured.

"Blasted barnacles, I placed my bet on Brownbeard," Stubbs said.

Scotty clucked his tongue. "A bad choice, for he's sure to go down in the rankings, and Rodney'll rise up."

Stubbs grumbled something unsavory under his breath.

Tricky sidled up to us. "I suggest we retreat to the ship. Things might get out of hand tonight."

"All the more reason to stay," Scotty enthused.

Quill sobered up immediately. "Aye, aye, captain."

"Not so fast." Scribbles stood before us, chin lifted, eyes directed over our heads. "Captain Olivia Twitchett Trickett of *The Pink Pearl*, the pirate king summons you and your entourage to an audience."

Chapter Eight

THE PIRATE KING was standing outside his tent when we approached. He waved at a group of pirates lounging nearby, his smile wide. "I swear by my magnificently barbaric beard I'll capture the culprit and make him walk the plank. Never you fear. I, your pirate king, am here to maintain an appropriate amount of disorder."

He waved us inside the tent, flopping onto another throne. "What a nuisance. It's bad for business, I'll not lie. I don't blame anyone for ridding the oceans of that nuisance. But why didn't they wait 'til *after* the parlay to kill Sweetie? I'd have given them a piece of gold or two for the service."

Tricky dropped into a high-back chair and swung her booted feet onto a low table. "These things do happen from time to time. Remember the fifty-first?"

Brownbeard groaned. "I'd rather not. Even with that, the current parlay might go down in history as the worst. I'll be walking the plank if I don't find the culprit. Worse, I'll lose my throne to that upstart, Rodriguez Montoya." He spat a heavy glob onto the canvas floor of the tent, then waved imperiously at Scribbles, who tiptoed over and wiped the spot clean with a dirty handkerchief.

"So why ask me here?"

I was beginning to wonder that myself. I would've been quite happy staying by the bonfire, but Quill had snagged my arm and dragged me after Tricky, Stubbs and Scribbles. "Can't leave you alone in this crowd," he'd said.

The pirate king tapped on his throne's armrests. "You didn't happen to—"

"No. I didn't kill him."

"Pity. Remember the support I gave you when you placed your bid for captainship? The first female captain ever. We made history."

Quill nodded. "Aye, and she's the best captain on the seven seas, I might add."

"Yes, yes. All of that." Brownbeard pursed his lips. "Truth is, you may be the only pirate here I can reasonably trust. Or rather, I don't completely distrust."

Tricky bowed her head ever so slightly, but her expression didn't change. She puffed heavily on her pipe. "You do have this handled, don't you, Brownbeard?"

The king groaned and pinched the bridge of his nose. "No! I don't. It's such an embarrassment. And mark my words, Rodney'll maximize the situation for his benefit. This murder... it puts me in a bad light. As if I'm incapable of keeping the peace during a parlay."

No one spoke, and the pause lengthened into an uncomfortable silence.

"Apart from Rodney, who else might benefit from this?" I asked.

The king's head snapped up, and his eyes narrowed in suspicion as he peered at me. "Who is this?"

"A blasted stowaway," Stubbs said. "Found her with the cannons."

"Why hasn't she walked the plank?"

"The chief," Quill and Stubbs said at the same time.

"Ah, yes. What'll you trade her for?"

"How about we focus on solving this murder," I say. "After all, we wouldn't want such a wise and benevolent—"

"You mean barbaric," Quill said.

"And barbaric king such as yourself losing your throne and your crown when the pirates vote in three days."

The king flared his nostrils. "Indeed not. I've had this crown for a decade at least. Imagine it on the head of that despicable Wee Rodney. You know what it means if he wins? His ma will turn the pirate parlay into a cooking contest." He shuddered.

Tricky tapped her pipe's mouthpiece against her front teeth but said nothing.

"All the more reason to determine our suspects, and investigate them," I said.

Pooky hissed. "You should keep quiet. Silence is a virtue, you know."

The pirate king's gaze sharpened. "You seem to know about this investigation business."

"Not specifically. That is, I read the newspaper from time to time. There are plenty of mysteries in there."

The king nodded, a frown squirreling between his eyebrows. "Right. I need this murder solved, and the culprit walking the plank before the election in three days. You do this, young stowaway, and I'll elevate your rank to pirate."

Quill gasped, Stubbs grunted, and Tricky tilted her head.

Pooky's claws dug into my arms. "Did I ever tell you I can't swim? If they make us walk the plank—"

I tightened my grip on Pooky. "I shall certainly do my best, your Barbaric Royalness."

"You better, or I'll announce you as the culprit."

"Me?"

Pooky mewed. "Why did I run away?"

"Yes, you." Brownbeard nodded. "Exactly so. You're a stowaway, so everyone'll believe it."

"Stowing away and murder are two very different sorts of crimes, wouldn't you say, sir?"

"A king doesn't need to answer his subjects. I shall declare you the murderer, and place Captain Tricky at fault for her lax security on her ship. Are we clear?"

Tricky narrowed her eyes at me, smoke curling around her face. "Crystal."

The king smiled and settled back in his throne. He smoothed his frilly cuffs and nodded. "Then you may leave."

We filed out of the tent. The beach was a study in chaos. An assortment of tents and hammocks sprouted up along the edges of the beach. A few even dared enter the jungle but not too far. Increasingly drunken pirates guzzled various liquids and shouted songs in clashing keys.

I didn't have much time to enjoy the scenery before Tricky stepped in front of me and exhaled a plume of smoke into my face. "You've landed us in a right mess, Miss Storm."

My gaze flicked to the side. Quill winced and shrugged his shoulders.

"I'm sorry?"

"Don't be sorry, Miss Storm. Be focused. Find who did this. Otherwise, we're all going down to the ocean's bottom. But I'll make sure you go first."

Chapter Nine

I FOLLOWED Tricky through the impromptu camp. Other pirates nodded at Tricky, some of them winking or giving a thumbs up. She didn't respond, but her arms swung harder as she quickened her pace.

"It seems they approve of you," I suggested.

Quill laughed softly behind me, but quickly stopped when Tricky glared over her shoulder.

"You're going to get us both killed," Pooky muttered. "And sharing one of my nine lives with you is *not* an option. But I shall suffer in silence as always."

"They think I murdered Rodney's quartermaster," Tricky said.

I jogged to keep up with her. She wasn't any taller than me, but somehow she strode faster than even Quill with his long legs. "Why do they think you murdered him?"

"I had issues with him."

My heart rate quickened. "What sort of issues?"

"Not the murdering kind, if that's what you're getting at. Many had issues with Sweetie."

"Of course." I let a question linger on the end of my sentence, unspoken but there.

"He didn't want me in the pirate brethren, not as a regular buccaneer, and definitely not as a captain. As quartermaster, he had a vote when I put my name forward for captainship."

"And he voted nay?"

Tricky harrumphed around her pipe. Puffs of smoke floated up, faster and faster as she sucked and exhaled. "That's right. He blackballed me."

"So you definitely had a motive."

Tricky twirled so fast, I collided with her. "What're you saying, stowaway? That I snuck away from the party and murdered that two-faced, good-for-nothing scoundrel?"

Quill chuckled. "No one'd blame you if you did. I bet Brownbeard's singin' your praises. Unofficial, mind you. Since officially—"

"Yes, perhaps unofficially," Tricky reluctantly admitted. "But only unofficially since officially this is a no-kill zone. I wish I could take the credit. That bloke was a sugar-stealing nuisance. He blamed everyone else, but he was the worst culprit."

I nodded sympathetically. Sugar was a precious commodity, only recently reserved for nobility and royalty. Now it was available for purchase but at a pretty price.

"But feel free to accuse me," Tricky added, her eyes narrowed into flinty slits. "I have an alibi. Then again, everyone does."

"Not everyone," I corrected. "The murderer had to be in the tent with the quartermaster."

Tricky shook her head. "Trust me. *Everyone* has an alibi."

I glanced toward the other end of the beach where Captain Rodney's crew had set up camp. The quartermaster's tent was very obvious. Most of the crew simply set up a hammock or a mattress with the intention of sleeping under the open sky. But quartermaster Sweetie's tent almost rivaled the pirate king's in size and elaborate decorations.

"Do you think they'll let me take a look inside the tent?" I asked.

Tricky's teeth clicked on the stem of her pipe as she studied me. "Aye. They'll have to now, won't they? Since the pirate king has appointed you as his lead investigator and all." Her lips turned up ever so slightly, and a plume of smoke curled out of her nostrils. "Seeing Rodney's expression... Let's go, then, Miss Storm." She spun around and marched rapidly toward Rodney's camp.

"You just had to offer, didn't you?" Pooky said. "What's wrong with life in a harem? The chief's wealthy, so we'll be set for life. I'll have lots of cream, and you'll have whatever chiefs give their concubines."

I tightened my grip on Pooky ever so slightly until he squeaked. "Not an option," I muttered under my breath.

"What's wrong with being the hundredth and one wife? You'll hardly see the man. It's the perfect marital arrangement."

I lifted Pooky and pretended to nuzzle him while I whispered in his ear, "I'm not being traded for camel milk. And I most certainly will *not* be one of a hundred and one wives or concubines or whatever he's going to do."

"Fine. Be that way. I suppose you'd rather walk the plank than live a life of royal luxury?"

"Pretty much."

"You sound more human by the minute. Disgraceful."

Quill looked back at me. "There a problem, miss?"

"So many," Pooky yelped. "Save me from witches with standards. So picky."

"No problem at all," I said and hurried after him.

I started making a mental list. Top of the agenda: solve this messy murder. Then help the pirate king win an election, and avoid joining the chief's harem. It was a pretty full agenda.

Tricky and Rodney were standing outside the quartermaster's luxury tent. Rodney's face was even redder than before, while Tricky looked almost pleased with herself. She nodded at me, and tipped out ashes from her pipe. They inconveniently floated onto Rodney's shiny boots. "Wee Rodney here has graciously agreed—"

"The name's Rodriguez Montoya," Rodney snapped. "You'll use me proper name, woman, or—"

"Wee Rodney!" An elderly woman's voice called out from the captain's tent. "I've warmed up your evenin' milk, love. Just as you like it."

Quill started to laugh but changed it into a loud coughing fit when Rodney placed a hand on his sword. Stubbs harrumphed. Tricky's mouth widened into what was definitely a smile now.

"Well, then." I nodded at Rodney. "I'll just get on with it, shall I?"

"Touch nothing," he ordered.

"Now, now, Wee Rodney," Tricky said. "Fair's fair. As the royally appointed lead investigator, Miss Storm'll have to investigate everything in there. Every. Single. Item. She'll have to open every box, every bag—"

"I get the point," Rodney said, his cheeks an unhealthy purple. "Be quick 'bout it. Me new quartermaster wants to use this tent."

"A replacement already?"

"Aye, can't run a ship without one. He was part quartermaster before, but I upgraded Winks."

"Part quarter," Pooky mused. "I feel there's a joke in there somewhere."

Tricky whistled. "How very unseemly. The poor man hasn't even been buried yet, and you've replaced him."

"The poor man…" Rodney blustered. "Aye, the poor man. Not to worry. We'll give Sweetie a pirate's sendoff."

"I'll need to meet with the new quartermaster." I forced myself not to flinch away when Rodney took a step toward me.

"That'd be me." A cheerful man stepped to Rodney's side, swept his hat off his head, and performed a small flourish with it. "Terrence Winks Wimble at your service. Call me Winks." His eyes squeezed shut, and his face contorted.

"What're you doing, sir?" I asked. "Are you alright?"

"Givin' you me famous wink, that's what." He opened his eyes wide, then sneezed several times. "Apologies, miss. I'm allergic to cats."

"He didn't just say that," Pooky hissed.

"And pretty much everything on this island. Tropical vegetation doesn't agree with me sinuses." Winks pulled out a handkerchief, wiped under his tearing eyes, then blew his nose.

I smiled sympathetically. "Not a fan of the great outdoors, then?"

"Oh, I'm a fan. A great fan. But jungles and cats aren't a fan of me." He sneezed violently again and hurried away, mumbling an apology.

"There," Rodney said. "You've met him."

"I'll need to have a proper chat with him. It's protocol, you see. Everyone's a suspect."

Rodney's face turned dark purple. "Everyone? Are you suggesting *I'm* a suspect?"

"Not you specifically. Just…" I shrugged. "Everyone."

"Let's keep her." Quill placed a large hand on my shoulder and squeezed. "She's very entertainin'."

Tricky bit down on the end of her pipe. "We'll see. Perhaps if she makes herself useful—"

"I'm sure *she* will," I said and entered the tent.

Chapter Ten

QUARTERMASTER SWEETIE'S tent looked the way the man did: prim and proper, all things put in correct order, and rather lifeless.

"I'm impressed he could unpack so quickly." I admired a collection of glass animals set upon a writing table.

"You think he did this? More like he had the cabin boy running around since the moment they landed." Tricky puffed on her pipe, strolling around the spacious tent.

"He's still here," Pooky whispered.

I turned around. "Who is?"

Tricky eyed me as if I'd sprouted wings. Her eyebrows pinched together. "The cabin boy. I don't keep track of all their names. He's not on my ship, so why should I care?"

"Quite right." But I was no longer paying attention to Tricky. Slouched in a chair in front of a small table was the murder victim. "They left him here."

Tricky smirked around her pipe. "You were thinking they'd already cleaned him up and carted him away? No one would've left the party to clean up this mess."

I swallowed hard. Witches lived for a very long time. I

had yet to attend a funeral. And I'd never had an occasion to see a human corpse.

"Feeling queasy, are we?"

There was no doubt about it. Tricky was smiling.

"No, not specifically."

"Methinks this be a new experience for you, Miss Storm." She pulled up the other chair at the small table and leaned toward Sweetie. "Imagine that, Sweetie. Looks like you finally have some effect on a young lady. Too bad you're not alive to enjoy it."

I sniffed at the implied accusation that my nerves were too delicate to handle the sight of a corpse. "I'll have you know my education included anatomy."

"Is that a fact?"

"It is. Grand… my grandmother ensured I dissected a wide range of species. I'm accustomed to handling and cutting up dead animals and organs."

"But it ain't quite the same when the dead thing's another human, is it?"

"I suppose not." I resisted the urge to cover my mouth or close my eyes. I focused on deep breaths. What would Tricky think of me if I displayed such signs of sensitivity and sentimentality?

More important, Grand Dame Puddlewick would be appalled if she ever learned a relative of hers swooned away at the sight of a bit of blood and a knife sticking out of a murder victim.

Just thinking about her disapproving scowl smacked me into shape better than smelling salts. I lowered my hand and studied the scene. I didn't focus on the knife, because there was only so much I could handle in one go. "It seems he was expecting company."

Tricky snorted. "Only company he liked was his own."

I took a step toward the small table. "Two cups and saucers. Unless he drinks for two, as well?"

Tricky chewed on her pipe's mouthpiece. "So you have eyes. You'll need more than them to solve this case."

"Why? Do you have any idea who it was?"

"Oh, aye. I do."

"Then why didn't you tell the king?"

"It could've been anyone. Hear me, Miss Storm? We're all suspects, like you said. We're pirates. It goes with the territory. And Sweetie here wasn't exactly a favorite among any crew, including his own."

"I see."

Tricky stood up and lifted the lid of an ornate wooden box. "Looks like he wasn't exaggerating. His sugar package is missing. Odd."

"What is?"

"I never knew him to drink tea without sugar. No wonder he was extra cranky this evening."

"What's that crest on the box?"

"His personal insignia. He stamped it on everything." She swaggered past me. "I'll be outside, when you've finished your *investigation*." Her emphasis on the last word told me exactly what she thought of my sleuthing skills.

The tent flap closed behind her, and I sagged in the chair across from Sweetie. "She's right. What do I know about solving a crime?"

Pooky squirmed out of my arms and flopped in the soft sand. "Who puts dirt inside their tent?"

"It's sand. Because we're on a beach. I think it's delightful."

"Appalling. Truly appalling. Life with Chief Ali Babak isn't looking so bad now, is it?"

I straightened up. I'd put up with all sorts of indignities as the granddaughter of Grand Dame Puddlewick. But everyone had a line beyond which they didn't step. And being the hundredth and one wife was right up there on my list of things I'd never do.

"No chief. No plank. We're going to solve this."

"I wonder if the chief has dogs? You'll have to get rid of them for me." The cat clambered onto the narrow bed and sniffed his paws. "Sand inside a tent. Despicable. Truly atrocious. What'll they think of next? Declawing cats? Putting a bell around our necks?"

"Perhaps." I looked at the tea set again. It certainly wasn't up to London standards, but for a pirate, it was probably a luxury. A small tin of powdered milk. A teapot with enough tea inside for two. "Where's the sugar?"

"There is none," Pooky said. "Weren't you listening to the pipe lady?"

"Exactly. She said he never drank tea without sugar. That's why he was so cranky today. So why would he set out tea for himself?"

"Why humans do the things they do is a mystery. Can we go now?"

I stepped away from the table and peered out of the tent. "Are you sure Sweetie never drank unsweetened tea?"

Quill and Tricky paused in their quiet conversation and stared at me. "Aye, never," Quill said. "He used to say tea without sugar is a crime he won't commit. You see how extra foul he was 'fore bein' murdered?"

Tricky smirked. "No doubt because his efforts to steal Rodney's stash were thwarted."

"He tried to steal his own captain's sugar?" I asked.

"Of course. Not openly, mind you. That's a marooning offense."

I pointed back into the tent. "Yet he set out cups for two people."

Tricky yawned. "As you already said."

I returned to the table. Both cups had dregs of tea at the bottom. I lifted the cup that wasn't in front of Sweetie and sniffed. I then took a tiny sip. It was cold and unsweetened.

"You done in here, Miss Storm?" Quill lifted the tent flap to peer inside.

"In a moment."

"She's definitely done," Pooky said. "Admit it. We're going to live with Chief Ali Babak and his hundred wives. I can think of worse situations, to be honest. He'll love me, of course. Royalty recognizes royalty."

"What's this?" I stooped to study small, white specks scattered across the table.

"Grains of sand, I imagine. There's so much of it."

"It looks like sugar. So where's the rest of it?"

"They finished it?"

"Sweetie said someone had stolen his package." I reached across the table, careful to avoid Sweetie's hands, and lifted his cup.

"I wouldn't drink that," Pooky said. "You've no idea where his mouth has been."

I set it down. "Good point."

"All my points are good bordering on brilliant, if I were to be honest."

"And so humble."

"Humility is for the untalented."

I delicately pulled out a handkerchief from Sweetie's pocket. "Excuse me, sir."

"No need to—" Pooky paused. "Were you talking to the dead man? Dear, me. This whole chief business has really shaken you up, hasn't it?"

"Hardly."

"What're you doing?"

"There must be a whole teaspoon of sugar here. Such a waste, and what a mess."

"Who cares? This isn't my tent, and cats don't eat sugar."

"Humans do." I swept the sugar grains into the handkerchief and knotted it in place. I then studied the corpse.

Grand Dame Puddlewick had ensured my education was thorough. While I never dissected a human corpse, I certainly studied the innards of various other animals. My tutor always went to great lengths to explain the similarities and differences between the animal in question and a human body.

"I think the knife isn't the murder weapon," I said, studying the wound.

"Humph! The knife's stuck in the middle of his chest. He's dead. I'd say the two are very much connected, don't you?"

"But there's very little blood around the wound."

Pooky did his version of a shrug, and whipped his tail up and down. "One less mess for someone to clean up. Is it dinnertime yet? I really feel it is."

I glanced at the tent door. It was closed. The candlelight was steady, as no draft came in to wobble it.

I shuffled my chair around the table until I was sitting almost knee to knee with Sweetie. "I'm so sorry to do this, sir."

"Again, enough talking to the dead guy. Talk to the live cat. Wait. What are you… No. You… Ugh! I can't watch."

Neither could I. I closed my eyes, gripped the handle of the knife and pulled. The knife came out with a squelching noise.

"Are you done yet?"

"I'm not sure. Can you check?"

"Absolutely not. You check."

I squinted through one eye. The knife seemed to float in front of me until I opened both eyes and saw my hand gripping it. "I did it."

"Yes, but why? Why would you do that?"

I swallowed hard and leaned close enough until I could see the skin on the other side of the torn shirt. "Just as I thought. Sweetie was dead before anyone used the knife."

Chapter Eleven

I WRAPPED the murder weapon that might not be the murder weapon in another cloth and exited the tent.

"Finally," Tricky huffed and glanced at the bundle. "A souvenir?"

"It's the knife, but—"

"Good. All we have to do is find a pirate who's missing his knife." She snorted. "Should be easy."

"Really?"

Tricky looked at me over her pipe. "No. Every pirate has at least one knife. It's going to be a chore to connect the murder knife to a specific person."

"I don't know. This knife's pretty unique." I unwrapped a bit of the cloth and stared at the handle. "It has a K engraved into it, surrounded by what looks like Arabic—"

"Stop talking." Tricky stepped toward me, her expression fierce and rigid. "Cover that thing up. Now. Hurry. Quill, we'll have to toss it right away."

I took a step back and clutched the knife. "Why would you do that? We need to find the murderer, and this is the one solid clue—"

"What's a solid clue?" Captain Rodriguez Montoya came around the tent. "Is that the…" He paused and thumped a fist dramatically over his chest. "I can barely say it."

"Then don't," Tricky huffed.

"I can barely contemplate a life without my steadfast Sweetie. So is that the murder weapon?"

"In a manner of speaking," I said.

"She's mistaken." Tricky stepped between me and Rodney. "It's a random object she found. The body's inside. We'll see you at the funeral."

"You said it's a clue," Rodney insisted. "Did you take something from Sweetie's tent?"

I stepped around Tricky. I didn't want to anger her, but her anger was better than a lifetime in a harem sharing a man with one hundred other women. "Yes. It's a knife with unique markings on the handle."

Quill groaned, and Tricky clamped her teeth tightly on her pipe.

"I don't think they like you," Pooky said and sat on my shoes.

"Let me see it." Rodney held out his hand.

"I'll share this with the king directly. He did ask me—"

"Don't your cooks sign everything with a *K* set in Persian designs, Captain *Olivia*?" Rodney stared down his bulbous nose at Tricky.

"Her cooks?" I glanced at Tricky, whose expression was darker than the storm clouds gathering on the horizon. "Oops."

"I demand justice," Rodney called out. "I demand the arrest of the guilty cook."

"It wasn't one of them," Tricky argued. "They're back at the ship. They aren't on the beach, nor were they when—"

"Um, captain?" Quill murmured.

"What?"

Quill tipped his head toward the gently rolling surf. A young man walked alone, his long black hair loose down his back. He stooped occasionally to pick up a seashell. He wore a long robe in a style I could only describe as Arab, even though he was Persian.

"Khalid, what're you doing here?" Tricky shouted.

The young, handsome man looked up, his gentle expression visible in the dim light cast by the large bonfire and a sliver of moon. His large, dark eyes shone under a solid eyebrow. His smile though brief was bright and cheerful. He jogged toward us, a large basket bouncing against his side. "Collecting shells to use at the grand feast, captain of my heart."

"Why?"

"To decorate the dinner plates."

Tricky flung up her arms. "Decorate the… Whose imbecilic idea was that?"

"Khalif. May my life be a sacrifice for him. He was desperate for seashells."

"How long have you been collecting shells?"

"I rowed over just after you did, commander of my soul. I have enough now. What's wrong?"

Distracted by the conversation, I didn't notice Rodney approach until he lunged forward and wrestled the blade from my hand. He held it up triumphantly like a trophy. "This is what's wrong. You, sir, are guilty of murder."

"What's this?" Pepe Le Pirate strode toward our group. "Found the murderer already, did you? Sooner than antici-pated, but well done, Miss Storm. Well done."

"I don't—" I began.

"Take him into custody, men." Pepe waved a hand imperiously to a couple of pirates trailing behind him.

"Our king'll be pleased to have this matter resolved so neatly. Although the whole affair still leaves a stain on the election and on my captain's honor, but what to do?"

"The thing is—" I tried again.

"Wait!" Tricky bellowed. Everyone froze, staring at her. "Khalid, is this your knife or not?"

Khalid looked at the knife in Rodney's grip, then at the growing circle of curious pirates. "Yes, my glorious captain. It's my favorite carving knife."

Several pirates groaned, and one muttered, "Figures he'd use a carving knife."

"Use it for what?" Khalid asked, his unibrow almost into his hairline. "Apart from carving up meat, that is."

Another groan.

"You're guilty," Rodney declared, his lips peeled back. "I demand justice on behalf of my Sweetie. We'll go before the king immediately."

Tricky held up both hands. "Rodney, you know this is ludicrous."

"You're right. Forget the pirate king. He allowed this to happen. We'll have a tribunal of equals immediately."

"Hurrah!" the pirates shouted, attracting more to the crowd.

"Now would be a brilliant time to leave," Pooky said, rubbing against my leg. "And don't forget to carry me. I've no intention of being stepped on by one of these brutes."

"I mean," Tricky called out above the excited chatter. "Khalid could never possibly murder anyone. He doesn't even like killing the fish we catch."

Khalid shuddered. "It's dreadful. Poor little creatures, flipping and flopping. I leave Khalif to do the deed."

"Who's Khalif?" Pepe asked.

"His twin brother," Quill said. "The two o' them

joined our crew after the last parlay. They look like mirrors of each other."

"Identical twins, then?"

"Don't know 'bout identical, but they look the same."

"All I know is my quartermaster was murdered." Rodney sniffed back a tear. "Justice will be done. I demand it!"

"Did you kill anyone with this knife or anything else?" Tricky asked.

Khalid shook his head, his eyes larger by the moment. "No, captain. Of course not."

"Of course he'd say that," Rodney said.

Pirates grumbled in agreement.

"It's the truth. I lost that knife shortly after landing."

"Hear that, mateys?" Rodney looked around, making sure everyone was paying attention to him. "He lost his knife. How convenient."

Pirates chuckled and nudged each other.

"But... but..." Khalid spun in a circle. He was surrounded by disbelieving faces. "It wasn't convenient at all. I'm telling the truth."

"The most unlikely story ever." Rodney gestured to a big brute with a heart tattoo on his exposed arm. "Toss him into the prison pit. He'll walk the plank at the end of the parlay."

"Captain, I didn't do it," Khalid shouted as a small swarm of pirates swept him away in the direction of the king's tent.

"I know, Khalid. I know," Tricky whispered.

Chapter Twelve

"Now that's all sorted." Pepe paused, his smile wide. "Any other questions?"

"Will there be a trial?" I asked.

"He's guilty!" Rodney said. "Already been proven."

"I have to agree." Pepe gazed around, making sure he had all of our attention. "Onto other matters. I'll have to ask everyone to stay out of Sweetie's tent until the funeral tomorrow. That includes you, Winks. I'll organize the proceedings, of course, as the king's too distraught. By His Barbaric Royalness' decree, Sweetie will rest in state until then, undisturbed. A guard'll be here at all times to ensure the lot of you stay out of his tent. Are we all clear?"

Muttered agreements met Pepe's orders.

"All right, then. Off you go. We have a busy schedule tomorrow. Wee Rodney isn't the only one who needs his beauty sleep."

"I definitely do," Pooky said and tried crawling up my leg. "Based on how everyone here looks, I'd say I'm the only one getting that sleep. Lift me up, please... Now carry me to bed."

Tricky gestured to me. "A word, Miss Storm."

"Don't go with the angry pirate lady," Pooky hissed in my ear. "Don't go, don't… And of course you go. Why do I bother?"

I followed Tricky to a quiet, uninhabited stretch of beach. The bonfire was a small smudge, surrounded by cheering shadows.

"A terrible way to start a pirate parlay," Tricky muttered.

"I'm sure Sweetie agrees."

Tricky glared at me. "You think my Khalid did this?"

"Is there another Khalid?" Pooky mumbled.

"I have no reason to say one way or the other," I said.

Tricky fisted the front of my shirt and yanked me forward. "Khalid didn't do it. Hear me?"

The tobacco in her pipe bowl smoldered. I tipped my head back to avoid getting scorched. Smoke curled up my nostrils and clouded my eyes. I wasn't sure if I should hold my breath, cough or beg for mercy.

"You find the real murderer, Miss Storm," Tricky said through gritted teeth, her voice soft and low and all the more dangerous for it. "You find him, or I'll make sure you pay the price. You understand?"

I nodded. "Find the murderer. Because Khalid could never do it. You're sure about that?"

Her fist tightened around my shirt. "Yes. More than certain. On my life, he's innocent. At least of this crime. He's a fine cook, a brilliant pickpocket, but he's no killer."

I decided to listen to Pooky's hissed warning and kept quiet.

"Now, I believe you need a few lessons in how to deal with pirates if you're to complete this investigation successfully. And by successfully, I mean clearing my cook's name."

"If you say so."

"Here's what I've learned over the years. This tidbit is worth gold, so listen up."

"I'm listening."

"If you're going to manage pirates…" She glanced around, then lowered her voice. "You have to know how to give 'em a solid glare."

"A… a glare?"

"Not just any glare, mind you. A *solid* glare. Right in the eyes."

"I grew up with my grandmother. I know all about good glares."

Tricky puffed on her pipe. "No offense to your elderly relative, but a landlubber's glare is a pale effort compared to what you need around these buccaneers."

I bit my tongue before I corrected Tricky. Grand Dame Puddlewick wasn't just any old *elderly relative*. She was a formidable water witch with centuries of experience in intimidation and curses.

"Show me what you have." She sat on a large, flat rock and waved at me.

"All this fuss over some stolen sugar," Pooky muttered and flopped down next to Tricky.

I called to mind Grand Dame Puddlewick's reaction when I told her I didn't want to marry Lord Percival Paaveling Wavily Moats. I'd never seen her so furious or outraged. I visualized her glare, her scrunched-up eyes, her scowl etching canyons around her mouth. Then I gave it to Tricky.

She yawned. "Really? That's all you have?"

I smoothed out my features, wondering if I'd forgotten something. Grand Dame Puddlewick used that ferocious expression to intimidate everyone in the Wavily Clan. Why wasn't it working on Tricky? She was a mere human. Most humans cowered before the wrath of Puddlewick.

Tricky puffed on her pipe. "Imagine the worst thing that ever happened to you. Go on. Dig deep, like you're burying a body. Get it in your head in gory detail. The gorier, the better. What're you picturing?"

I thought about that. What was the worst thing that had ever happened to me? "I suppose being forcibly engaged to a man I haven't met ranks high on the list. The month Misty and I spent in the dungeon together. That was pretty nasty. My sister's younger than me, and—"

Tricky coughed a laugh and shook her head. "I see I have my work cut out for me."

"You and me both," Pooky said. "I like the pipe lady. Why aren't you a pirate, too?"

"Try copying this." Tricky lowered her pipe, narrowed her eyes and suddenly turned into a horrifying caricature of a human.

"Gracious!" I shrank back, wondering if she was about to pull out her sword and spear me with it.

Tricky chuckled. "That's what I'm talking about. You need to refine a look."

"Truly, I'm astounded," I gasped, trying to calm my scratchy lungs and slow down my racing heart.

"As you should be."

"You want me to perfect a look like *that*?"

"Yes. The look you give wayward pirates when they're misbehaving. What did you think when you saw me just now?"

"You were going to impale me."

She tipped her pipe toward me. "Exactly. You were a few seconds away from a painful demise. That is what you need to put into your personal *La Look*."

"My look."

"No. *La* Look. The one no soul ever wants to face alone. That's how I became the first female pirate captain. Try this. Imagine you've been so gravely insulted by an upstart, impertinent man that you're one heartbeat away from pulling out your saber and stabbing him in the heart. Repeatedly."

"That was graphic," Pooky said and curled up on Tricky's lap.

She stroked him while studying me. "You *do* have an imagination, don't you? Or are you a typical London lady, fit only for needlepoint, marriage and pregnancy?"

My cheeks flushed, and I channeled my outrage into my face. "How dare—"

"You almost had it there." Tricky pointed at me, smiling around her pipe. "That one. It's not a bad first attempt at a *La Look*."

I touched my face with both hands. It felt the same to me. No fangs jutted out of my mouth. No volcanic liquid oozed from my eyes. No horns on my head, either. "Really?"

"Like I said. Not bad. Let's try it again. This time, combine eyebrows, your mouth, your eyes, your nostrils. Every part of your face must be involved in the glare. With one look, you promise a world of agony to the unfortunate recipient. Can you do this?"

"Yes?"

She puffed at the pipe, rings of smoke circling her head. "You don't sound very convinced. If you can't convince yourself, how do you expect to convince anyone else?"

"Yes. Yes, I can do this."

"Prove it. Try again."

She made me practice repeatedly until my face was exhausted. I'd never had an exhausted face before. By the end, she seemed pleased with my progress. "It's a good start, Miss Storm. Keep it up. You might just get there one day."

I smiled, pleased by the compliment. "Thank you. I shall."

"Now, I believe it's supper—"

"Finally," Pooky meowed.

"And then time to catch us a murderer."

Chapter Thirteen

WE SPENT the night on *The Pink Pearl*. Tricky was taking no chances. The cease-fire had been broken before it'd even started, and she gave everyone a lecture before dinner.

"Keep your swords sharp, and your wits sharper. We don't want a repeat of the fifty-first, now do we?"

Muted nays drifted around the deck.

"That's it. Lecture over." She glared at the circle of pirates. "You can eat now."

"Ahem."

Tricky clamped her teeth on her pipe. "Yes, Stubbs?"

"Lord's prayer. Ye promised."

"Is it Friday already?" Tricky seemed to bat her eyes in feigned innocence, but I assumed that was a trick of the dim lighting. As impressive as my imagination was, I couldn't imagine a pirate, and a captain no less, batting her eyelashes at one of her crewmembers.

"Aye, it is."

She smiled sheepishly. "It must've completely slipped my mind, what with all the excitement of a murder and the pirate parlay."

Stubbs jutted out his chin. "Slip or no, it's what we agreed. Friday night dinner. The whole blasted crew eats together, an' says a blessin' together. Like ye promised."

"Get on with it, then, matey," Scotty said. The sailing master licked his lips. "Some of us're wanting to eat 'fore next year."

Appreciative chuckles joined Scotty's booming laugh.

Stubbs' scowl deepened. I didn't think that was possible. And it definitely wasn't the dim lighting cast by storm lanterns hanging from ropes and masts.

"Where's Khalif?" Stubbs asked, looking around the table.

"He asked to be excused," Tricky said. "He's in a pretty bad state, what with his twin being arrested."

"Cap'n, with respect," Stubbs said and knocked a fist on one of the tables scattered around the deck. "Traditions are important. An' Friday nights're our tradition. 'Tis the only time we break bread all together as a crew 'stead of in shifts."

"Absolutely, and I'm going to give him a pass just this one time. Considering all that's happened, it's okay to have a bit of leniency from tradition. Shall we begin?"

Stubbs' face turned a strange shade of bruised purple, and it sounded like someone was choking him. He finally nodded. "Aye, aye, cap'n. Right, then. Close yer eyes, ye heathens."

"Only if McCormick promises not to steal me taters," Monks said.

McCormick, the master gunner, frowned at the young boy. "How 'bout I steal your whole plate? You wee scoundrel."

Monks' smile widened. "Yes, sir."

"Kids these days," McCormick grumbled good-naturedly.

"Still want to eat sometime today," Scotty said.

"Don't feel right without Khalid here," Monks said, his smile wilting.

Several of the other pirates nodded.

"We have a plan to prove his innocence," Tricky said. "Don't we, Miss Storm?"

A silence settled across the deck, and the pirates all stared at me expectantly.

"Can I eat now?" Pooky asked.

I forced a smile. "Absolutely."

"About time." He began slurping at a bowl of porridge.

"Oi! Friday night prayer." Stubbs glared at us. "Close yer blasted eyes."

"How reverent," I said.

Tricky whispered under her breath, "Stubbs is all about tradition. No getting around it. Tradition, and his church."

"Which one?"

"I never thought to ask."

Stubbs began a prayer in a monotone voice, and we stopped talking. I shooed Pooky away, and he meowed persistently. Stubbs prayed louder, and Pooky started howling.

"And Lord, save Khalid's soul an' bless us, amen," Stubbs said. "And do somethin' 'bout that blasted cat!"

Pooky leaped onto my lap. "Did he just pray for me?"

"Something like that," I said.

Between the lengthy prayer and Khalid's absence, a subdued mood settled over us as we ate. It didn't last long.

"Hey, Scotty," Clarke said. "You fixed the anchor winch?"

"Good question," Tricky added. "Did you?"

Scotty huffed. "Oi! Cap'n, I'm a sailin' master, not an engineer."

The other pirates laughed, and I waited for someone to explain the joke. As no one did, I assumed it was another longstanding tradition and focused on eating.

"How're you gonna catch the real murderer, Miss Storm?" Monks asked around a mouthful of mushy food.

"Mouth closed when you eat, lad," McCormick grumbled.

"But it's a good question, ain't it?" Scotty said.

The pirates were again staring at me.

"Yes, Miss Storm. Do tell us your plan." Tricky leaned away from me, as if to separate herself from whatever might happen next.

"First, I… Well, I shall make a list of suspects." It sounded like a good idea once I said it, and I felt better already. "Yes, that's what I'll do."

"Grand idea," Scotty said. "Who's on the list? I'm bettin' our captain's on it."

"Hurrah!" the crew cheered.

"Seriously," Scotty continued. "Who wants to make a wee wager on the matter?"

Tricky frowned. "Not now. Am I on the suspect list?"

I stared in any direction that wasn't hers. "Of course not."

"Whatcha mean, o' course not?" McCormick asked, stabbing his knife into the table. "You think our captain ain't good enough for thievin' and murder? Least of all, riddin' us o' that sugar fiend?"

Other pirates muttered unhappily.

"No, not at all. That is to say—"

"So you don't think she is, or you do?"

"No, I mean yes. She's perfectly capable of committing a perfect murder."

"Are you accusing me of murder?" Tricky asked.

"You can't win this one," Pooky said.

The cat had a point. "No, I'm not accusing you of *this* murder, although I'm sure you're able to flawlessly execute a murder without leaving any clues."

Tricky's gaze sharpened, and Quill leaned toward me.

"What clues?" Monks asked.

"I believe I'm going to sit somewhere else," Pooky declared. "Far, far away from you. Their pistols aren't very accurate. And there's only so many lives a cat wants to lose at one time."

I straightened my back and lifted my chin. I didn't plan on facing a pirate firing squad with bad posture. "As it so happens, I do have a clue."

"Oh, that's good news," Scotty said.

Stubbs grunted wordlessly.

McCormick nodded. "Aye, it is. Well, then. Let's eat."

"Okay." I hesitated, knowing I should follow Pooky's hissed directions to say nothing. "The thing is, Sweetie died before he was stabbed."

There was a moment of silence on *The Pink Pearl*. Drunken shouts echoed across the water from the beach. As per the pirate king's orders, we had remained in the harbor along with the other ships. The bonfire had settled down to dim embers, but that didn't stop the pirates on the beach from carousing loudly around the pit.

"The knife didn't kill him, then?" McCormick asked.

"Correct."

"He wasn't murdered by no knife?" Stubbs asked.

"That's right. He—"

Scotty jumped up. "Place your bet on what actually killed him, mateys. Maybe twas the sugar!" He collapsed in his chair, laughing.

The pirates joined him, guffawing at my attempt to explain. Scotty leaned so far back, his chair tipped over. He crashed to the floor and laughed harder, encouraging the other pirates to laugh both at him and me.

"No, I'm serious," I protested.

"This'd be a good time to use your La Look," Tricky said.

"They have to be looking at me, and able to see me clearly for it to work," I argued. "They're laughing too hard."

Scotty straightened his chair and sat down, wiping tears of mirth from under his eyes. "Oh, lassie, you're a strange one, you are. Stowin' away on a pirate ship. Talkin' to your wee cat."

"She be a witch," Stubbs muttered.

"Then claimin' a man don't die when he's stabbed with a knife."

I reached over to a candlestick and pounded its base against the table several times. Wax splattered across the surface. "Listen up, buccaneers. When somebody's stabbed to death, there's a lot of blood around the wound. Sweetie's shirt was barely stained. Which means his heart had stopped beating when the murderer stuck him with a knife. Any questions?"

The laughter vanished, and Scotty eyed me with something approaching grudging respect. "How'd you know all that?"

"Oh, maybe she's an assassin!" Monks shouted. "She's all nice and pretty, talkin' good with the man, then *bam!* Stabs him in the heart."

I coughed delicately and took a sip of water. "I commend you for your imagination, but no. I most certainly am *not* an assassin."

"Then how you be knowin' all o' this?" McCormick asked.

"Grand... My grandmother. She made sure I had a

thorough education. I dissected animals, studied various weapons and the like."

"And who did you say your grandmother is?" Tricky asked.

"I didn't."

Quill grinned and placed an arm across the back of my chair. "You're a different sort o' landlubber, ain't you, Miss Storm?"

"I suppose that's true."

If they had any idea how true that was, I'd either be hailed as a hero, or tossed off the boat with weights attached to my ankles.

"You should be a pirate."

"I have other plans, thank you."

Quill shrugged. "Plans depend on the wind, and if the tide takes you there or no."

"I prefer not to rely solely on climatic inclinations."

"So who be your suspects?" Monks asked.

Again that breathless silence, a sense of expectation.

I cleared my throat, scrambling for ideas. "Well, certainly not our captain. She wouldn't have left such a glaring clue."

"Hurrah!"

"The pirate who first found Sweetie." I paused, mulling over the abrupt and excited announcement. "It could've been him. He killed Sweetie, then rushed over to announce it. He'd be the last person anyone would suspect."

"Yeah. That stinker," Monks said.

"What was his name?" I asked.

"Just said it. Stinker."

"His name is…" I instinctively rubbed under my nose. "Well, him. I have to add him to the list."

"How long is your list?" Scotty asked.

"Not too long. I'm still working out who might have a reason to kill Sweetie."

Tricky chuckled. "Everyone."

"No, I mean who benefits from it."

"Again, everyone."

"But is there anyone who would specifically benefit?" I asked, desperate for a list that included more names than simply Stinker.

"Rodney's new quartermaster," Quill said.

I snapped my fingers. "Exactly. The new quartermaster. And while the murderer could be anyone, Winks benefits the most by getting a promotion."

Tricky nodded, sucking on her pipe thoughtfully. "Good point. Quill, I want you to accompany Miss Storm tomorrow in her investigation."

Quill grinned and winked at me. "Absolutely my pleasure, captain."

"Very kind of you, but it really isn't necessary," I said, yanking my chair out of Quill's embrace.

Tricky smirked. "I beg to differ. You're still working on your *La Look*."

Quill whistled, and Monks gasped.

"The captain's teaching you how to make a look?" Clark asked, his blue eyes wide.

"Yes?"

The pirates glanced at each other, not meeting my gaze.

"Still a work in progress," Tricky said. "As I said, Quill, stay close to Miss Storm."

The smile widened, and he winked again.

I cleared my throat. "Actually, I might have better luck unaccompanied. You know, people might open up to me—"

Laughter burst out around the table.

"They sure will open up to you," Tricky said. "Quill will be staying by your side, all the same. Oh, and Quill? Pack a tent in the morning. I want our guest of honor staying on the beach tomorrow night. Miss Storm needs to find more clues."

Chapter Fourteen

I TOSSED AND TURNED, trying to find a comfortable position. It didn't help that I was surrounded by barrels, crates and bags of food supplies in various stages of freshness. Or that my mattress had what was certainly a thriving colony of bed bugs. And I didn't want to think what was on the itchy blanket.

"Are you going to fidget all night?" Pooky asked. "Some of us like to sleep."

"I just might."

"Then go outside."

I forced myself to lie still, but my mind tossed and turned instead. What if I couldn't solve the murder? What would happen then? I was more worried about Tricky than the pirate king.

Thunder rumbled overhead, an echo to my anxiety. Rain slashed across the porthole, and restless waves slapped against the hull.

"Are you worried?"

I blinked into the darkness. I sensed rather than saw a

face close to mine. I reached out and swatted it away. "No."

"You should be." Pooky nestled next to my neck. "I mean, assuming you still aren't up for being wife number one hundred and one?"

"Absolutely not."

"I thought so." A pause. "Even if they have lots of cream and sardines?"

I stroked his head. He really was a pretty cat. "Even if they had all the cream and sardines in the world."

"Too bad. I guess that settles it."

"Settles what?"

"I'll help you solve this case."

"How generous of you, Pooky."

"My parents almost gave me Generous for my middle name."

"Imagine that. So what do you think we should do first?"

"Breakfast, without a doubt."

"Of course. I wouldn't imagine launching an investigation without tea and other sustenance."

Pooky sniffed, and his whiskers tickled my nose. "You aren't such a bad witch after all."

"I'm considered a promising talent among my peers."

"There's no need to boast about it. Remember who's descended from a cat goddess, and it's not you. Then we'll take a nap."

"You want to take a nap first thing in the morning?"

"Of course not! How outrageous. We'll nap first thing *after* breakfast. Were you not listening? Perhaps you have hearing problems. I didn't consider that." He pressed his muzzle against my ear and shouted, "Can you hear me?"

I pushed him away. "You're only cute when you're *not* shouting at me."

"I'm not aiming for cute. I'm aiming for divine."

"Hmm. I suggest we skip the after-breakfast nap."

"No!" He pounced on my chest and pressed his face against mine. Now both sets of whiskers were tickling me. "Tell me you're joking. Surely you jest."

"I suppose humans and witches don't need as much sleep as cats do."

"You do realize great brainpower requires a lot of sleep? It's why cats nap so often. To allow our prodigious brains a rest."

"I'll keep that in mind. What are you doing?"

"Purring, of course."

"I realize you're purring. But why are you doing it while sitting on me?"

"To relax you, so you can go to sleep." He nestled his head under my chin.

"You're not such a bad little fellow, after all."

"You do realize I'm doing this for purely selfish reasons?"

"If you say so."

"I do. Go to sleep. Or do I have to hypnotize you again?"

"You've never hypnotized me."

"There's a first time for everything. Look into my—"

"Continuing with our planning."

Pooky yawned. "I plan to nap."

"After breakfast, we'll go to the beach."

"What a frightful place. All that sand, sun and surf."

"Yes, how will you manage?"

"I'll suffer in silence."

"Really?"

The cat flexed his claws. "Of course not. Fine. We'll go to the beach. And then we'll collect the teacups and test the contents for poison."

VERED EHSANI

"Poison!"

Pooky sighed. "Perhaps you have selective deafness. That must be it. Yes. *Poison*. And I'm not talking about the tea leaves, as ghastly as those are. Why do humans ruin a perfectly good cup of warm milk? It boggles the mind."

"As boggled as your mind is, tea is an elixir among beverages."

"Humph."

"But back to the poison. What do you mean?" I reached into my bag, fumbling for my matches. I lit a candle and stared at Pooky.

"Goodness, are you blind as well? It was perfectly bright enough in here without that candle."

"Pooky. What poison?"

"The one in the tea, of course. Surely you sniffed it out? That's why you picked up the cups. Wasn't it?"

"How do you know what poison smells like?"

Pooky puffed out his little chest. "Because I'm Sir Dedrick Bartholomew Pocock O'Doherty the Third, descendent of the cat goddess—"

"Yes, yes. But it makes sense."

"That I'm related to divinity? Of course. I'm a cat. What did you expect?"

"I mean about the knife. And the wound not being that bloody. I suspected he died *before* the stabbing. But I didn't know from what. It must have been in his tea, not his guest's."

"You're welcome."

I flung off the dingy blanket, no longer tired. "We need to get back to that tent, before someone like the new quartermaster goes in there and cleans out the cups."

"I bet he did it."

"Who?"

Pooky blinked at me, his yellow eyes large. "Whoever inherits the luxury tent from the dead pirate, of course."

"I thought of that."

"Only after I mentioned it."

"Naturally. Maybe we should go back there now—"

"Now? As in immediately? In the middle of the night?"

It was my turn to sigh. "It's hardly the middle of the night. What if I'm too late? My first real clue, and maybe it's been washed away."

"Didn't the distinguished pirate—"

"You mean Pepe?"

"Yes. That one. Didn't he say the tent was off-limits until after the funeral?"

"He did."

"So there's your answer. We can't go."

"But will that stop the murderer from returning to remove any evidence? No, it won't. Assuming it was poison."

Pooky scoffed. "Assuming? Did I not say it was poison? Then you rest assured, young witch, that poison it was. Really, you doubting my abilities is a cruel blow. Cruel!"

"My apologies. Are you ready to go?"

Pooky's shoulders slumped. "I suppose I owe the young cook my best. He did give me a brilliant lunch yesterday. Not to mention an amazing back scratch."

I stood up. "Then we're agreed."

"I hope this isn't one of those situations where I'll have to remind you I told you so."

I scooped him up. "What exactly did you tell me?"

"You'll find out when something goes wrong."

"And on that cheery note, let's go find that poisonous tea."

Chapter Fifteen

THE ROWING BOATS the crew had used to get to shore were still bobbing by the side of *The Pink Pearl*. The rope ladder was also conveniently left in place. The worst of the storm had passed, leaving behind small, choppy waves and a heavy mist. I even managed to climb down the ladder without skinning my palms or falling.

I jumped the last foot into the closest rowing boat, landing heavily on one ankle. The boat tipped heavily to one side, water sloshing against my arm as I tried to right myself.

"This isn't so bad, after all," Pooky said from his perch on my shoulders.

I collapsed on a bench and rubbed my ankle, hoping I hadn't twisted it or broken something. "Speak for yourself."

"I only ever speak for myself." Pooky clawed down my back and flopped next to me. "Who else would I do it for?"

"Silly me."

"Going somewhere, Miss Storm?" a male voice called out.

"She kidnapped me!" Pooky yowled. "I had nothing to

do with this harebrained scheme. Save me. And don't make me walk the plank!"

"What a traitor," I muttered, then looked up.

Quill waved, his grin wide and relaxed. "Tryin' to run away, are you?"

"Yes, Quill. That's what I'm doing. I'm running back to London. In a rowboat."

"'Tis a long way."

"Which is why I'm rowing."

"Shouldn't you be enjoyin' a good night's rest first?"

"I should, but alas. I find myself requiring a before-bed stroll. Sadly, the deck is far too small."

"So you fancied a midnight rowing session instead?"

"Indeed. I find it a most refreshing constitutional after such a heavy meal."

He nodded, his expression turning thoughtful. "You wouldn't happen to be goin' to the beach, now, would you?"

"If the tide takes me there."

He didn't smile, and I wondered just how much trouble I was in.

"It's not safe to go there by yourself, not for a young lady."

"What about the peace accord?"

Quill smirked. "Ask Sweetie how that worked for him."

"Good point. What're you doing?"

"I think it's obvious what he's doing," Pooky said. "He's climbing down the ladder. He'll either toss you over his shoulder or into the ocean. Such a savage. It's been nice knowing you."

"Comin' with you, o' course," Quill said, landing gracefully in the boat without tipping it. "Can't have our favorite stowaway gettin' herself into trouble, now can we?"

"You have any other stowaways?"

Quill paused as he set the oars. "Can't say we ever have. Don't think too many people are brave enough to hide inside a pirate ship."

"In my defense, I thought you were just merchants."

"Aye, that we are, among other things. You 'bout scared Stubbs into a fit, poppin' up among the cannons."

Oars splashed softly through the water, a soothing rhythm to it. I smiled as I thought of my first meeting with Stubbs. "How did he lose his leg?"

Quill lowered his voice into a conspiratorial hush. "'Cause o' the Nandi Bear."

"A what bear?"

"Nandi. It's not a bear."

"But you said it was."

"Aye. East Africans call 'em Kerit. Looks like a cross 'tween a giant hyena and a bear. Most unnatural thing you can imagine."

"I suspect that's exactly where it can be found. In one's imagination."

Quill winked. "There you'd be wrong, Miss Storm. The Nandi Bear, it's real. And it was one that ate Mr. Stubbs' leg. He be lucky that's all it ate. Their preferred meal is human brains."

"Brains?"

"Aye. Bigger, the better. And it don't care much how smart they are. So losing a leg ain't half bad, now is it?"

"I'm all astonishment."

"And well you should be. But don't you worry, miss. They're found in the Rift Valley mostly. We're safe enough this far north."

"I'm beginning to wonder how safe I am anywhere these days."

The waves settled into ripples as we approached the

shore. The party was finished, as was the bonfire. The only sound were the oars sloshing through the water, and Quill's soft breath as he guided us to the beach.

"Do you mind if I ask you a question?"

Quill winked at me. "You just did."

"Another one, then. Why did you join the pirates?"

For the second time in as many minutes, Quill's smile faded. "Wasn't my first idea for a profession, I'll tell you that."

"What was?"

"My pa figured I'd help my brothers when they took o'er the farm from him. But bein' the youngest of seven brothers—"

"Seven! My heavens."

"That's what my ma said when she weren't chasin' after us for our misdeeds. It wasn't a bad life, bein' a farmer. A bit too routine, though."

"Isn't there a routine on the ship?"

"Aye. That there is. But there's also a lot o' change. Change o' scenery. Change of activity when we're 'bout to board a ship, or fightin' off those trying to board us. Constant adventure. More to my taste, if I'm bein' honest."

"Which I hope you are at all times."

He laughed, and I felt myself smiling with him.

"So you like the adventure. Is that why you joined?"

He chuckled. "Not exactly. I was kidnapped."

I gasped. "Kidnapped? By pirates?"

"Aye."

"I can't imagine Tricky doing that."

"No, not her. Another crew. I was but a lad. They needed a new powder monkey, bein' as their previous one didn't last out a battle. So there I was, a wee lad, learnin' 'bout cannons and such. Not much older than Monks."

I had to remind myself to breathe. "And then what happened?"

"They picked a fight with the wrong ship. Tricky and her crew made short work o' them. She offered amnesty to whoever swore loyalty to her and signed *The Pink Pearl*'s Codex. Figured I'd be better off with a lady cap'n than the brute who kidnapped me."

"And were you?"

"Without a doubt."

I was sitting on the edge of the plank, the rough wood digging into my thighs. "You didn't want to return to your family?"

"Not really. Tricky offered to drop me off near their village, but by then I fancied myself a pirate more than a farmer. Life on *The Pink Pearl*'s been good to me. Now I'm the quartermaster, second in command. Not too shabby, for a farmer's boy."

"Farming isn't that bad."

"No. But as the youngest of seven, I didn't have a chance o' inheriting any land. I'd be working for one o' my brothers, or some other farmer. Always have a master, instead o' bein' my own. Didn't sound like a life I wanted."

I looked away. "How true."

"What's your story?"

Pooky purred loudly and crawled onto my lap. "Careful. He's digging for info. Information is gold. Or rich cream. Valuable, either way."

"Not much to tell."

Quill clucked his tongue. He paused in the rowing to wipe his brow. The boat bobbed on the small waves. "Fair's fair. I told you my story. Honest and all. I'm sure you have one. A pretty young lady such as yourself, wanderin' 'round unaccompanied at night in dodgy places, climbin' into a pirate ship—"

"I didn't know that at the time."

"Don't matter. You knew well enough all sailors are men, Tricky bein' a rare exception. And men're dangerous enough without them bein' pirates. You get it?"

"I certainly do."

"So?"

I shivered as I thought through the implications of his words. Quill was right. I hadn't considered the danger before. I was lucky the captain was a woman who'd taken pity on me, or at least offered to give me a chance. "I wasn't really thinking, to be honest."

"Which you always are, right? Honest, that is."

"Somewhat. I was running away from an arranged marriage."

Quill whistled and shook his head. He resumed rowing. "Must've been a terrible match, then, Miss Storm."

"She didn't even know the bloke," Pooky said. "Translate for me."

"It's not that. I just… I prefer to choose my own life. To be my own master, if you will."

Quill studied me, his rowing smooth and uninterrupted. His eyes glowed with an intensity I found both uncomfortable and intriguing. "Aye. I well understand that, Miss Storm. We're here."

Sand scraped against the bottom of the rowboat, and Quill leaped out, splashing through the surf as he dragged the boat higher onto land. He held out a hand to help me out.

"What a gentleman." I allowed him to help me.

"Bein' a pirate don't mean we can't be gentle. Now, what's the plan?"

I looked down the beach. The mist was too thick to see more than a few feet in any direction. "I need Sweetie's teacups."

"I didn't take you for a thief."

"Not to keep. I just want the contents."

Quill tilted his head in the direction of Sweetie's tent. "As per Pepe's instructions, Rodney's put an honor guard outside. I think he don't want anythin' stolen until he has a chance to pilfer it first."

"Then I guess we'll have to find a way around the guard."

Quill's smile brightened the darkness. "Now that's somethin' a pirate can help with."

Chapter Sixteen

"I THINK HE LIKES YOU," Pooky said and rubbed against my legs, almost tripping me.

"Stop it," I whispered, shooing Pooky away with a gentle swat.

"I'm a feline. I smell things."

"Poppycock."

"I'm telling you. He's into you. You have my permission."

"How generous of you."

"You're welcome. Now pick me up. You know how I feel about sand under my claws."

"That cat sure meows a lot," Quill said as he led me along the edge of the forest.

"Tell him he should learn to speak cat," Pooky said.

"Yes," I agreed. "He certainly is a noisy little beast."

"Keep him quiet, Miss Storm. We don't want to wake anyone."

I wrinkled my nose. "It smells like everyone is too intoxicated to wake up for anything less than cannon fire."

Quill looked back at me, winking. "That's a point."

"A noisy little beast," Pooky muttered. "I'll have you know I'm descended from royalty."

I didn't bother replying. Instead, I scoured my mental list of spells that I'd perfected. I had a fair number, especially given my youthful age. But I'd never worked with seawater before, and the small vial of freshwater wouldn't last very long if I needed more than one or two spells. I needed to practice with saltwater. I promised myself that if I wasn't traded for camel milk, I'd focus my energies on doing just that.

"Only one guard," Quill murmured and dropped behind a rocky outcropping.

I knelt next to him, close enough to hide but making sure to keep a bit of distance. Pooky's comments had unnerved me. Quill was pleasant enough, and certainly not lacking in physical attractiveness. I might need him as an ally if Tricky was true to her name and sent me to the chief after I solved the mystery. But I wasn't ready to commit to anyone until I knew I was safe from Grand Dame Puddlewick.

"Here's the plan," Quill whispered in my ear, his breath tickling my neck. "I'll knock the guard senseless, and you run into the tent and get what you need."

"Or we could distract the guard with noises. While he runs around investigating them, I could sneak into the tent and grab what I need."

"Not bad. Not bad at all. But knockin' someone unconscious wasn't part o' the king's forbidden list. So I'm not breakin' the pirate parlay's peace accord by thumpin' the guard on the head."

"I'm not sure the pirate king will let you off on that technicality. He might categorize such an aggressive maneuver under dueling and fighting."

Quill sighed. "Very well, Miss Storm. It shall be as you say. Who'll make the noise to distract the guard?"

I turned to Pooky and nudged him with a finger.

"Absolutely not. Do you seriously expect me to run around like a small lunatic, being chased by a larger lunatic? And on all this sand?" The cat shuddered. "My poor claws. What they've endured."

"I can toss your cat into a bush," Quill offered. "That'd make a lot o' noise."

Pooky hissed.

"Why don't you tell the guard you found someone sneaking around the tent," I suggested. "You then lead him to investigate the situation."

Quill's grin returned. "Sneaky. I like what you're doin' there. Tellin' the truth. Ingenious."

"I never thought of telling the truth as ingenious, but I can see why you'd think that. Yes, I'm being devilishly sneaky."

Quill gestured to me to stay down. He jogged away from the tent, then reappeared lower down on the beach. Mist swirled around him. "Oi, matey! I found us an intruder! Tryin' to get in the tent."

I didn't hold out much hope, but the ploy worked. After a breathless exchange, the guard followed Quill into the jungle.

"Stand watch, Pooky," I ordered.

"No promises. I'll stand. I may watch. But I'll probably take a nap instead."

"Then at least stay out of my way. Stop trying to trip me."

"Can I help it if you're clumsy?"

I jogged to the tent, my shoulders tense. At any moment, the guard was going to realize he'd been tricked and run back in a fury. Was he allowed to use his sword on me?

Nothing happened.

I slipped inside, fingers crossed the evidence would still be there. It was dark, and I was tempted to leave the flap open. But what if Rodney or the guard walked by and saw it open? They'd certainly investigate.

I pulled out my precious vial of freshwater, placed a few drops in my hands, and cupped my hands. "*Double, double toil and trouble. Night burn, and eyesight double.*"

The water glowed blue. Bright tendrils of steam drifted up, swirling in front of me until they coalesced into a small ball of light. It was the best I could do without attracting attention. Anything brighter, and someone was sure to wonder at the sudden appearance of light in the darkened tent.

"It's over here," Pooky said. He was already next to the table, sniffing delicately. "It still smells like something bad."

"It could be the body behind you."

Pooky looked over his shoulder and screeched. "They really left him in here? Savages. The least they could've done was toss him overboard or on the sand. Those little crabs would've taken him away."

"Yes, that's much more civilized." I took out two flasks I'd borrowed from the galley and poured the contents of the teacups inside. One flask for Sweetie's cup, one for his unknown guest. I made sure to scrape out the dregs, just in case the poison had left a sediment.

"Are you done? This place gives me the creeps." Pooky sidled up to me and pressed against my leg.

"I think that's it."

"Can we go now?"

"You didn't strike me as the squeamish sort."

Pooky glared up at me, his yellow eyes reflecting the

light from my small globe. "It's a dead body! Of course I'm squeamish. You should be, too. What's wrong with you?"

I scooped him up, holding him close.

He nuzzled against my neck. "Let's never see another dead body again. Are we in agreement?"

"That sounds like a marvelous plan. Shall we?" I extinguished my light and tiptoed to the tent's entrance, then froze.

"I swear to you. He's just o'er there," Quill argued.

"Don't see nothin'," the guard muttered. "And Rodney, he told me ta stay here. So I's stayin' here."

"But whoever's sneakin' around must be the murderer. Don't you want to be the one who captures the murderer?"

There was a pause, and I held my breath.

"Nah. I's all good. Let the king find the murderer. It be his job."

"That's a point. A game o' cards?"

"Oh, yes. Sure be borin' out here."

"Then let me entertain you. Wait. What's that o'er there? Stop, don't—"

"What? What's it?" the guard asked.

Quill gasped. "Look, the intruder. Behind you. Watch out!"

"Where be the fiend? I'll…"

A soft thump interrupted the men, and something heavy landed against the tent. The canvas buckled slightly, then a human-shaped form slid off.

"Miss Storm?"

I ducked outside and stared at the unfortunate guard lying face down in the sand. "Really? He knew you were here. You'll be blamed for this."

"Nay. Didn't you hear my story?" Quill tossed a thick branch toward the jungle and brushed his hands together. "I saw the intruder who attacked this poor man. Tried to warn him, I did, but too late. The intruder thumped him heavily."

"And conveniently left you alone, I take it?"

Quill hesitated. "He didn't see me 'cause o' the heavy mist. I ran after the fiend." He jogged on the spot. "I did my best but lost him in the jungle."

"And then you slipped quietly away, leaving your friend in the sand?"

"What friend?"

"The one starting to wake up."

"Quick, hide. I'll deal with this."

I started to retreat. "I hope you're right."

Quill winked at me and pulled out a flask of potent-smelling liquor. "I'm always right. That's why I'm the quartermaster."

"Omniscient, are you? I'll make sure to tell God he has competition."

Quill frowned.

"Because you claim to know everything... Never mind." I ducked behind the rock formation, clutching Pooky and listening to Quill convince the guard of his dodgy story.

The two men searched the area for the attacker, then gave up the hunt to play several rounds of cards. The guard won every round, and Quill gave him a celebratory swig each time. By the time Quill joined me, the guard was snoring loudly.

"That'll do the trick," Quill said. "He won't dare say a word 'bout tonight."

"How clever. Can we go back to the ship now?"

"Was it there?"

I gripped the flasks through my pocket. "It was. Which makes me wonder. Why didn't the murderer clean up after himself?"

"Because he didn't know you have an amazing cat as your companion," Pooky said and waddled after a hermit crab scuttling across the sand.

"Perhaps."

Quill nudged me with his elbow. "Perhaps what?"

I forced a smile. "Perhaps I need a good night's rest, after all."

Chapter Seventeen

I WAITED until Quill left me in the pantry before pulling out the flasks and the handkerchief of sugar.

"You aren't going to do more work at this time of night?" Pooky asked.

"That's precisely what I intend to do. I have to test the poison. Depending on the type, it might degrade and be unrecognizable if we don't hurry."

Pooky yawned. "You work too hard. All this running around has exhausted me."

"Then feel free to stay here."

"I shall. Where are you going?"

"The galley."

"The what?"

"The kitchen. I need ingredients for——"

"The kitchen? Why didn't you say so!" Pooky rolled off a low shelf and plopped down beside me. "I'm always ready for a trip to the kitchen."

"Although I believe it's called a galley on a ship."

"It's the same thing. A blissful source of food."

"Let's hope we're the only ones going for a midnight

snack."

Pooky swished his tail as we padded down a narrow corridor. "I'm sure there's enough food to go around. I'm happy to share."

"How generous of you. Here it is."

The galley was a tight space, like everything on the ship. Every vertical and horizontal surface was put to good use. Herbs hung from the ceiling on hooks. Preserved vegetables in jars lined the back of the countertop. Everything was cleverly tied down with strips of leather.

Pooky used a set of shelves to climb up to the countertop where he collapsed, wheezing and huffing. "Find me some of that leftover fish. I'm dying here."

"You shouldn't be walking on the counter. It's not hygienic."

Pooky froze. "It's not? You mean they don't wash this place properly after cooking? Why didn't you tell me before? Humans. You can't rely on them to do anything right."

"I meant... Never mind." I set down my storm lantern and lit a small fire in the wood stove.

"Are you going to burn the poison?"

"Of course not. But since we're here, a cup of tea wouldn't go amiss."

"What about my leftover fish?"

I rummaged around in the cool box. The pirates didn't leave a lot of food uneaten, but there was a bowl of congealed fish scraps. "Kalif is probably using this in our soup tomorrow."

Pooky sniffed disdainfully. "What a waste of a decent fish head. Over here, please. On a porcelain plate, if you don't mind."

After sorting out Pooky's midnight snack, I searched for my ingredients. Grand Dame Puddlewick was an expert on poisons, a skill she shared with her granddaughters. My mother had little interest in the subject matter, and my stepmother had been horrified to learn about my curriculum.

But it came in handy. Potions and poisons were a decent enough business for any self-respecting witch. Grand Dame Puddlewick had taken pains to remind me of the fact almost every time she gave me a lesson.

I studied the ingredients before me. "We have almost everything except—"

"Is there a problem?"

I gasped, almost dropping a small bottle of vinegar as I spun around. Khalif stood in the doorway. His long black hair was unusually messy as if it hadn't seen a comb in a day or two. His general appearance was disheveled, which wasn't like him. The few brief interactions I'd had with him had impressed on me how particular he was about his appearance.

"Just making some tea." I slid in front of the ingredients.

Khalif yawned, rubbed his eyes and tried to smooth down his rumpled hair. "I'll join you, if you don't mind. I can't sleep, knowing Khalid's in that darksome pit. How he must despair."

I nodded sympathetically, wondering if I should offer to make him tea and bring it to him. It wasn't what a proper lady would do. Then again, I was hardly proper, and these were trying times.

"Hello, gorgeous one, delight of my heart." Khalif tickled Pooky under his chin.

Pooky purred loudly, his tail whipping back and forth. "Now this is a human I can tolerate quite easily. See how he adores and worships me? Scratches me in just the right locations? I hope you're taking notes, witch."

"I pray to the heavens Tricky doesn't send you to the chief's harem," Khalif said. "But if she does, may I keep your cat?"

Pooky rubbed his head against Khalif's hand. "You absolutely may."

"He's not really mine to keep or give away," I said. "You'll have to ask him."

Khalif smiled, a sad upturn of his finely shaped lips. "I appreciate how you treat this cat as if he understands us."

"And I've downgraded my assessment of him." Pooky wrinkled his nose.

"Hmm. Tea. Chamomile?" I pulled down a jar of dried chamomile flowers.

Khalif leaned against the counter and eyed the ingredients behind me. "What're you doing with all of those?"

"Those… yes, those. I'm making a treatment for the cat."

Pooky's head snapped up. "I hope you're not serious."

"You're serious?" Khalif said.

"Absolutely. The poor little beast has worms."

"I most certainly do not!" Pooky howled.

"A strange set of ingredients to manage worms," the cook said. His dark gaze sharpened.

"You're right." I held up the flasks. "I'm testing for poison, actually."

Khalif hopped onto the countertop. "Your cat's been poisoned?"

"No. But I believe Sweetie was."

"You mean *I* believe he was," Pooky said. "Tell him it was my idea."

"But what about Khalid's knife?"

"It was placed at the scene *after* the murder."

Khalif gasped. "That means Khalid definitely didn't murder him!"

"Exactly."

Khalif's smile widened, and a twinkle came to his eyes. "You'll prove him innocent, then."

"That's the plan."

"Thank you! You know a lot about poisons?"

"A thing or two. It's a hobby, really. My grandmother's the expert."

"Your grandmother sounds like a pirate."

"More like a witch, but I'm sure she'd make a good pirate, too."

"You should tell the captain you know about poisons. That'll increase your status in her books."

"I'd rather not be in her books at all."

"And if you find out it was poison? What then?"

An excellent question. I still didn't have many suspects, and one was already in the pit, awaiting execution. "I suppose I'll search everyone's belongings for traces of poison."

Khalif laughed. "No one'll let you do that."

"Don't look at me," Pooky grumbled. "I'm done with exploring other people's tents. The last one stunk, and it had a dead body in it. It's shocking how people leave bodies lying around hither and thither."

"First things first," I said. "I need to identify the poison, if there is one. Then I'll see who's the most likely candidate for using it."

"Stinker knows a thing or two about poisons," Khalif said.

"You mean the pirate who found Sweetie dead? That's convenient if true."

"It is. Ask anyone. Although his list of poisons is limited. Still, he's a good suspect to start with."

I nodded, mentally adding a star next to Stinker's name

on my list. He seemed more and more likely to be the candidate I was looking for.

"But it definitely wasn't my brother," Khalif said.

"So I've been told. And it was *definitely* poison." I gestured to the three small pots I'd set on the stove to simmer. "The one on the left was the contents of the guest's cup. As you can see, it's still purple."

"And the other two?"

"The sugar grains, and Sweetie's tea."

"Pink means poison?"

"It does in this case. Whoever killed Sweetie must've stolen his sugar first, coated it with poison, then returned it to him. At that point, Sweetie put on a tea party, as he promised he'd do."

Khalif sniffed at the steam coming off of the pots. "Do you know what the poison is?"

"I do."

"Really? You're extraordinary, Miss Storm."

"Not at all. The reaction and resulting color give it away. It's an unusual poison made from a night flower called *Decaying Corpses*."

"A horrific name."

"For a horrific smell. It's definitely not a flower one wants in one's home. But the poison is odorless."

"Flowers make my brother itch."

"That would present a challenge while preparing the poison. So now we're looking for a suspect who has both motivation and some expertise in flora."

"A strange thing for a pirate to know," Khalif said.

"I suppose so. There's only one course of action left for us. We shall have to search everyone's belongings."

"No captain'll let you do that, Miss Storm."

"Which is why I won't ask."

Pooky groaned. "This isn't going to end well."

Chapter Eighteen

DESPITE THE CALM WATERS, I wasn't able to sleep very well. And I couldn't blame my stomach for the unease.

Why would someone use a knife *after* poisoning Sweetie? To shift the blame to Khalid? But why him? It made no sense. Then again, the past few days made no sense. I'd run away from one problem, only to land into another.

Talk about hopping from the pan into a pot of hot tea. It was only getting hotter.

I reflected on the harebrained idea I'd shared with Khalif. It had sounded like a perfectly reasonable plan in the moment. A murder investigation naturally required the investigator to rummage through suspects' personal belongings.

But Khalif was right. No one was going to give me permission, which meant I'd be sneaking into the private quarters of ruthless pirates. What would they do if they caught me?

"Pooky, are you awake?"

"Why do people ask that question? If I answer you, then obviously I'm awake. And if I don't—"

"Yes, yes. Why kill someone with poison, then fake a stabbing?"

"Humans are a strange and incomprehensible species. Can I go back to sleep now?"

"I suppose. Do you think maybe he didn't trust the poison? Or maybe he had a grudge against Khalid. Or—"

"I hear humans think much better after a good night's sleep. It's certainly true for cats."

"I don't know how you can sleep."

"Quite easy, actually. Do I need to teach you how to sleep, as well? Simply close your eyes, close your mouth, and stop thinking."

It actually wasn't bad advice, so I tried it. The next thing I knew, someone was kicking my feet.

"Pooky, stop bothering me," I mumbled into what passed as my pillow.

"Miss Storm, we have a problem," Quill whispered.

"Only one? It can wait until after morning tea."

"Someone may've seen us on the beach."

I rolled over and squinted against candlelight. "Who? So what?"

"You always so foul first thing in the mornin'?"

"I am when someone rudely awakens me without offering me so much as a cup of tea in apology. Now how do you know someone saw us? Apart from the guard you knocked out, then allowed to beat you at cards."

Quill smirked. "You figured it out, eh?"

"I can't imagine he could've won much after that concussion."

"Aye. You have a point."

"Fine, I'm awake." I rubbed my eyes and started to sit

up, then realized I was in my nightgown. "Do you pirates not have any sense of propriety?"

"Property? O' course, and it's all ours."

"Never mind. Who saw us, and why is it important?"

"Squidly."

"Our Squidly?"

"The one and the same."

"How could he have seen us? It was dark and misty."

"He's tellin' the captain right now he saw a rowboat headin' for the section o' beach where Sweetie's tent is."

"He's not wrong. Did he actually identify us, though? Or the boat?"

"Nay. I'm just warnin' you. If Tricky asks, we weren't there."

"We weren't where?"

"On the beach, at—" He stopped and reluctantly smiled. "I see what you did there."

"Splendid. Can I please get dressed now?"

"Excuse me." Khalif pushed past Quill. "You're still asleep, Miss Storm? My apologies. And who messed up the sardines?"

"Time to skedaddle," Pooky said and waddled out of the pantry.

The ship was abuzz with the news of midnight skulking and possible thievery. Scotty could barely contain himself. "I'm tellin' you, it's that scalawag Captain Rodney. Who'd like to place a small wager on the matter?"

McCormick strolled into the dining area and straddled a bench. "Why does he bother stealin' what's already his, man?"

"His ma set him up to it. Tryin' to make the pirate king look bad."

"Don't have to try too hard."

Monks bounced on his seat. "It's how all coups begin. Murder."

"You know he's not really royalty," I said and reached past Clark to snatch a piece of toast. "He's like everyone else here but with a bit of metal on his head."

"Oi, mateys!" Clark thumped the table with a hand and laughed. "Look who's soundin' like a pirate?"

"Hurrah!"

I bit back my smile. "Not at all. Besides, why would anyone want his job? It's just an honorary position, right?"

Clark wiggled his hand back and forth.

"Honorary position it is," Quill said. "With a few perks an' benefits."

"How'd you think he funds the pirate parlay? We all give him tribute after the election."

"An' he sure don't spend it all on the blasted parlay," Stubbs grumbled.

Tricky swaggered into the small mess hall. "You lot still here scarfing down food? The games are about to begin. Miss Storm, Quill, you're with me. The rest of you sea dogs, up and be done with it."

I exchanged looks with Quill, and hurried after the captain. She waited until the three of us plus Pooky were on one of the smaller rowboats. She pinned a glare on me, then puffed a heavy smoke ring. "I know it was you."

"What was who?" Quill asked, his innocent expression marred by a flinch as Tricky leaned closer.

"Find anything useful?"

"We might have," I admitted.

"Good. Remember: tonight, you're on the beach. I want you investigating each and every pirate there. Scout their tents. Pick their pockets."

"I was hoping for a more subtle approach," I said.

Tricky scowled and spat into the water. "I don't care if

it's subtle, blatant, hit 'em over the head with a hammer. Just prove Khalid didn't do it."

"We're working on it."

"Work faster."

The parlay activities were well on the way when we scrambled up the beach. Sword-tossing competitions and stick battles were popular. The anchor-dropping event required sailing masters to prove their accuracy by dropping an anchor through a ring. There were cannon range and accuracy tests. And it was all scheduled to happen before lunchtime.

"Goodness," I said as we passed an event involving knives, blindfolds and a dead fish. "Aren't some of these a tad dangerous?"

Quill nodded enthusiastically. "Aye! 'Specially that one o'er there."

"The apple-bobbing contest?"

"People've near drowned."

"While bobbing for apples?"

"The honest truth."

"As I've never heard of dishonest truth, I'll take your word for it."

Quill snatched an apple and offered it to me. "At least no one's lost a limb yet, but the fifty-first... Best not speak of it. We don't want to jinx ourselves."

"People lose limbs?"

"Not very often."

Pepe Le Pirate, the pirate king's quartermaster, hurried over to us. He ignored Quill and bowed to me. "Miss Storm, the pirate king has instructed me to take particularly good care of you today. Would you care for a tour?" He held out an arm, and hooked it around mine.

I glanced back at Quill, who shrugged.

"I take it this is your first pirate parlay," he asked as we veered around a wrestling match involving three pirates and a pigskin.

"Yes. Indeed it is."

He stopped abruptly. An anchor plunged through the air a few feet in front of us, thumping in the center of a ring on the sand.

"O'er the X," a pirate shouted from a tree branch. "Bullseye! Full points for—" The limb snapped, and the man tumbled down, landing heavily next to the anchor.

"Yes, Hubert," Pepe said. "It certainly looks like a bullseye."

The event's audience hooted and jeered. The referee scolded Hubert for slowing down the proceedings, then dragged him out of the ring and gestured to another man to climb the tree.

"Do you think he needs medical attention?" I asked.

"He hasn't lost a limb, so I say no. Look at this. I never did understand this contest." Pepe gestured to the row of barrels filled with water and a few bobbing apples. "What pirate worth his stink puts his head underwater? You know most of us buccaneers are deadly scared of drowning."

"Yes, I imagine most people are."

"But most people don't face it as an occupational hazard."

"That's a good point."

"Are you still convinced Khalid isn't guilty?"

I hesitated. "I'm keeping my options open."

"How goes the investigation?"

"Slow."

Pepe nodded and patted my hand. "Don't worry, Miss Storm. I have faith in you. You'll figure out who broke the peace. It'd certainly put my captain at ease. Poor man. He's desperate to keep his crown."

"So I heard. But doesn't he want a break from such a lofty office? It must be tiresome."

"'Tis a burden, indeed."

"Then would it be so unbearable if another became king?"

Pepe looked around, as if checking to make sure no one was close enough to hear us. "I think not. It'd be better for his health. Then again, I'm not the one in charge here, am I?" He laughed. "Truth is, pirates claim to love chaos, and we certainly seem to thrive on it. But the king provides a sense of stability and tradition. Someone who can resolve difficult disputes and such. The crown is held with the greatest respect and not to be treated with disregard."

A loud meowing snagged my attention. Pooky was halfway up a tree, clinging to a branch. His fur stood out, making him look fluffier and fatter.

"Fascinating. It's been a pleasure chatting with you, Pepe. I believe my cat needs some assistance."

He lifted my hand, and I was about to yank it out of his grip in case he tried to kiss me. But he didn't. He simply bowed, dropped my hand and backed away. "You'll let me know if you need any assistance, won't you, Miss Storm? My captain's happiness and well-being rely on it. On you, in fact."

"Of course."

Pepe walked away, a spring in his step. He paused to cheer at the efforts of a pirate escaping the hangman's noose tied around his wrists. One of the contestants had already escaped, and another was well on his way. But the third was clearly having no such luck.

"What a strange lot this is," I said, tugging Pooky off the branch.

"It's about time you rescued me."

"Why did you climb up in the first place?"

He glared at me, his eyes unblinking. "What sort of a question is that?"

I returned to the ship to pack a few items for the night's adventure. Quill rowed the boat for me.

After a few minutes of silence between us, he asked, "What did Pepe want?"

"To offer me assistance. He also gave me a tour of the games."

"Don't trust that so-and-so," Quill warned. "He looks after his own self, that's all."

"Don't we all?"

Pooky fidgeted in my arms. "I should hope so. Talking about looking after one's own, we'll get some cream, won't we?"

I opened my mouth to answer when someone screamed.

"Now what?" I muttered.

We were gliding toward *The Pink Pearl*. A pirate was clinging to the end of a boom halfway up the tallest mast.

"There's always one in every party." Quill shook his head. "You'd think they'd figure out how to walk on narrow poles without slipping."

"Help! Get me down!" the pirate screamed.

"Just jump, Squidly," one of his crewmembers shouted. "Ye be needin' a bath, anyway."

Other pirates laughed and jeered from the surrounding ships.

"Lads, get a net under him," Quill shouted.

"Why?" Clark shouted back.

"'Cause I can't swim!" Squidly squealed right before his hands lost their grip, and he plummeted toward the ocean.

Chapter Nineteen

"DON'T DROWN," Quill shouted, the speed of his rowing increasing.

"Can't... help... it," Squidly blubbered as his head bobbed under the soft waves.

"If you get closer, I'll snatch him up," I said.

"He's rather rotund," Quill grunted. "You think you can manage?"

"And he doesn't have the excuse of fluffy fur," Pooky added.

I shrugged off my jacket and shoes. "What sort of sailor doesn't know how to swim?"

"The normal kind," Quill said.

I leaned over the side of the rowboat, preparing to do my best. At least I could keep the man's head out of the water until Quill reached my end of the boat.

Pooky sat next to me, peering at the struggling man. "What sort of water witch doesn't use her magic when they're in the water?"

"The kind who doesn't want to be found out by a

shipload of sword-wielding, gun-carrying pirates," I said under my breath.

"An excellent point. Then we let him drown?"

Pooky was right. Squidly had disappeared under the waves, and wasn't reappearing.

"Blasted barnacles," Stubbs shouted from the raised forecastle at the bow. "He gone an' drowned again."

"Guess we lost him," Quill added, closing his eyes and making the sign of the cross.

"Aren't you going to jump in there after him?"

"So two of us can drown?"

"Unbelievable. I should think the first training sailors receive is how to keep their heads out of water."

Quill shrugged. "Poor Squidly. He was a good man. Well, not really. But he was a very good pirate."

"Really?" I patted my pockets, removing a few items.

"No. He was a terrible pirate. But he was always good for a laugh."

"Hold onto these." I pushed my jacket and shoes into Quill's arms and stood on the edge of the rowing boat.

"What're you thinking? You're tippin' the boat."

"I'm going to save Squidly." Ignoring Quill's shocked outburst, I dove into the ocean.

The pirates' shouts calling for me to get back faded as water surged around me. All water witches knew how to swim. We could also hold our breath far longer than humans. It was practically an innate ability. So I wasn't concerned about drowning. But finding Squidly was a whole other business, one requiring a bit of magic.

I'd never used saltwater before, but there was only one way I could find Squidly in the murky waters. I began to burble the words into the water, precious air bubbles blowing out with every syllable.

"Double, double toil and trouble. Fire burn, and cauldron bubble. Bring us back from dark to light. So we may see so bright."

It wasn't nearly as effective as chanting the spell above water, but I couldn't risk Quill or anyone else seeing what was about to happen.

At first, nothing happened. The salt obstructed my magic. I tried again, putting all of my focus into the words. The intent was more important than the actual spell.

This time, a trickle of glowing blue current weaved through my fingers before darting ahead of me into the depths.

I followed it down, hoping I wouldn't have to go too far. I was happy to save Squidly, but not at the risk of drowning. I'd already used up some of my air in speaking the spell, and I hadn't yet mastered how to breathe under-water. I added that to the growing list of things I needed to do if I survived my time on the pirate ship.

A flutter of cloth caught my attention, and I swam toward it. Squidly was still struggling and flailing. His efforts were weakening, and his eyes were closed. I kicked harder, willing Squidly to slow down. Or better yet, maybe kick so he could come toward me.

Instead, he stopped moving and began to sink faster.

Of all the ungrateful creatures. Here I was, risking life and… well, life, and he gave up?

Infuriated, I swam faster, using my arms to propel me. I stretched out, and my fingers grazed against his hand.

His eyes jerked open, and he gawked at me, precious bubbles trickling out of his mouth. He ignored my head shake and started to panic. More bubbles exploded out of his mouth.

Quill was right. Squidly was a terrible pirate.

I grabbed his hand, this time getting a firm grip. I turned myself around and began kicking hard.

But Squidly was no small man. He made up for his humble height with his excessive weight. And he was wearing boots which were weighing him down like matching anchors. I wasn't going anywhere except down.

I needed to speed things up. *"Double, double toil and trouble. Fire burn, and cauldron bubble. Speed of dolphin, fin of fish. Breath of night and time by third. For a charm for making double. The feet they fly out of trouble."*

Glowing blue water swirled around my legs, solidifying into a long fishtail. I could still feel my legs, but now they had a powerful aide. I gave myself a mental clap on the back for achieving a rather complex spell. And in saltwater, no less! What would Grand Dame Puddlewick say about that?

Squidly sagged against me. I hugged him close and began to whip the glowing blue tail back and forth. In a few brief moments, we broke the surface of the water, gasping for breath.

"They're alive!" Clark shouted from the deck.

"Hurrah!"

Quill reached down and pulled Squidly into the rowboat, where he lay gasping and limp like a stranded fish.

"Your turn, Miss Storm." He stretched a hand toward me.

I was about to accept his offer of assistance when I realized I had a small problem.

My fishtail still surrounded my legs.

I did a quick mental check. How long did the spell last for? The answer: it depended. It always infuriated me when Grand Dame Puddlewick told me that. It depended on the witch's abilities, the spell's power, the circumstances, and a long list of other elements like the position of the moon to the earth, the time of day, and if the witch had just eaten breakfast or had been fasting.

I had no idea how long I was stuck with the fishtail.

"Actually, I feel like swimming some more." I pushed away from the rowboat.

Pooky hissed. "I thought you died down there. Do you know what that sort of trauma does to a cat of my sensitivity? You unfeeling creature."

"Miss Storm, that's a bad idea," Quill said. "What if you get tired? Or cold. Or you miss midmornin' tea?"

I gulped. It was tea time, and I desperately needed a cup. Or three. But I couldn't risk it. The pirates had been decent enough so far. Seeing a fishtail around my legs might give them reason to suspect I was more than a stowaway.

"Miss Storm!" Tricky shouted from above.

I leaned back, swimming away from Quill's grasping hand. "Hello, captain! It's a fine day for a swim, isn't it?"

"It's never a fine day for a swim. Now get in that rowboat, and come up here at once."

"I'd love to do that," I said. "But—"

Tricky leaned over the main deck's guardrail. She was too far away to do anything about my disobedience, but close enough to give me her La Look. The look alone should've frightened the fishtail off of me. Instead, it solidified it even more.

"Do go on, Miss Storm. Please give me one good reason why you should remain floating around down there?"

"Well… I… skin fungus. I have a skin fungus."

Pooky hid his head under his front paws. "I can't watch this. Wait, you have *skin fungus*? And I let you pick me up?"

"Skin fungus," Tricky drawled. "Really."

"Yes. Really. It's terribly itchy. It flares up in times of stress."

"And I suppose ocean water makes it better?"

"Absolutely. It heals it better than any ointment. I'll be good to go in no time at all."

Quill squirreled up his face. "It's not… you know… spreading, is it?"

"Oh no, it's a genetic issue. I inherited it from my grandmother. On my dad's side. It's not contagious at all."

"A cage what?"

"You can't catch it," I said.

Quill exhaled heavily and smiled. "That's good. Well, I'll leave you to your swimming."

I glanced down. The glowing blue fishtail was still there. "Please do. Nothing like a constitutional swim."

Quill chuckled, and put the oars to good use. "You're a very strange young woman."

"You have no idea," Pooky said.

Chapter Twenty

QUILL WAS RIGHT. I did miss tea time. And Khalif had made crumpets and jam.

"Of all the miserable luck," I grumbled as I collapsed on the deck. My clothes were plastered to me, and my hair stunk of fish.

"And it was delicious," Pooky said as he sauntered toward me.

"Thanks."

"I'd let you hug me, but you're wet."

"Again, thanks."

"And you have a skin fungus." He pawed at the deck. "I was worried, you know. It's not a good look on me, so don't do that again." He pressed the tip of his nose against my cheek.

"I'll try not to."

"Oi! She stopped swimmin'!" Clark called out.

Pirates appeared as if from thin air. Sliding down masts, jumping off booms, stepping around barrels, popping out of coils of rope.

"We had a bet goin', didn't we, mateys? On how long you'd last out there," Scotty announced.

"Hurrah!"

"Who won, Scotty?"

The sailing master grinned. "Think that was Squidly. He's got quite a thing for our pretty stowaway. What that she saved him an' all."

"The day keeps getting better," Pooky purred.

Squidly came up from below deck. "Aye, she saved me. Did more than the lot o' you, she did. Show some gratitude."

"Hurrah!"

"Your enthusiasm would mean so much more if any of you bothered to save a scone for me."

The pirates quickly took an interest in whatever they'd been doing before.

"That figures."

"There ain't no more scones, miss," Squidly said. "But I can fetch you a cuppa, that I can."

"Please do."

Squidly grinned. I really wish he didn't. The man had black stumps for teeth, and a lot of gaps in between. "I'll go fetch it at once."

I leaned back and closed my eyes, grateful the sun was warmer than in London. Even still, it would take a couple of hours to dry my clothes, and I hadn't packed a lot. A spare shirt, a dress just in case, and the pantaloons I was wearing.

"You've made quite a spectacle of yourself," Tricky said.

I squinted up at her. "Is this the thanks I receive for saving your crewmember's life?"

"Useless heroics."

"It wasn't entirely useless. He's still breathing."

"True. I suppose we should thank you."

"You're welcome."

"Get up, then. We have a meeting with his Royal Pain."

I glanced down at my pantaloons. I was sitting in a rapidly growing puddle, one that Pooky was careful to avoid. "Right now?"

"That was the order. Right now, unless you have something better to do?"

I sighed. "A cup of tea?"

"No time."

"How about a dry shirt."

"That'd be preferable."

I squelched below deck to my room in the pantry. I wrung out my pantaloons as best I could, and changed my top. There was nothing I could do about my shoes, which was a pity. They'd been a birthday gift from my mom, shortly before she'd left. I'd always liked them, even when they were too big for me. And eventually they fit just right. Now the onslaught of sun, sand and sea had ruined them.

"I suppose I'll have to do without." I left my poor shoes on the deck, hoping they'd look better dry, and clambered down the rope ladder into the rowboat.

"Barefoot?" Pooky sniffed at my toes. "You smell like a dead fish. I have nothing against dead fish. In fact, I rather like to consume them. But only when they look like fish."

I shooed Pooky away.

"I saw a rat in the galley today," Tricky said.

"Good for her," Pooky said. "Tell her she should really set rat traps. What sort of a ship is she running here? Such shoddy captaining. It's a wonder it still floats."

"I'll make sure my cat deals with it at once," I said, ignoring Pooky's outraged hiss.

"He doesn't look like much of a rat catcher."

"You're quite right," Pooky said. "I don't look like one, because I'm not one. Chasing rats. Humph! What has the world come to?"

The tide was with us, and we reached the beach quickly. Quill dragged the boat onto the sand, and started to offer me his hand. "It's really not catchable?"

"What isn't?"

Pooky dug his claws in my arm. "Mushrooms."

"Oh, that. I think you should be safe. The salt cleared up my skin completely."

I jumped onto the sand and paused. My feet sunk into the softness, and I relished the experience.

"First time, eh?" Quill studied my feet with an unhealthy interest.

"It's rude to stare at a woman's ankles." I tugged my pantaloons lower, but they did nothing to cover my legs past mid-shin.

"Can't help but notice. You're not wearing shoes."

I hurried past him, catching up with Tricky, who marched across the sand in knee-high boots. "How do you manage this lot?" I muttered.

"La Look. That's all."

I suspected it was more than that, but I said nothing as we entered the king's tent. He sat on his throne. On one side stood Scribbles, a long scroll gathered in his hands. Pepe, Rodney and his new quartermaster Winks waited on the other.

"All of the suspects are here," I whispered.

Tricky looked at me, almost giving me her signature look.

"Well, well, Miss Stowaway," the pirate king said as he brushed at his frilly frock.

"It's Miss Storm," I said.

"And what of the investigation? Have you found anything new?"

Rodney huffed. "This's a waste of time, your Barbaric Highness. We already have the murder weapon, and the murderer in custody. What can she tell us?"

"A lot," Quill blurted out. "In fact—"

I kicked Quill's leg. It wasn't very effective, given I wasn't wearing shoes, and he had muscles everywhere, but he stopped talking. "A moment of your time, sir."

"Do proceed."

"Actually, if you don't mind, I'd rather discuss my investigation in private."

Scribbles cleared his throat loudly. "You're addressing the king."

"What? Oh, right. In private, your Majestic Bearded One."

"What you have to say to me can be said to everyone here."

"With all due respect, sir—"

"Such a waste of time," Rodney said.

"It's not a waste of time, if we capture the real culprits." Tricky paused. "Wee Rodney."

Pepe sniggered.

Rodney's face flushed an ugly purple. "Only my ma is allowed to call me that."

"Carry on, Miss Storm." Brownbeard gestured with his hand.

Pooky gave a cat shrug. "He's the king. And I have no intention of walking the plank with you. So tell him!"

I sighed. "Well, sir, it was poison."

"What was?" Brownbeard glanced at Scribbles. "Are you taking notes? Good. This'll juice up my memoirs. What was poison?"

"The murder weapon, sir."

Rodney choked on a cough. "Poison? What sort of… Ridiculous. It was the knife. We all saw the knife in my poor Sweetie's heart."

"Yes, and that knife was stuck there *after* Sweetie died from poison."

Tricky almost smiled around her pipe. "Perhaps the knife was put there to make us believe Khalid did the crime."

"That's a possibility," I said. "Either that, or the murderer wanted to make sure Sweetie was dead."

"Poison!" Rodney spluttered. "Rubbish."

"It does sound improbable," the king agreed. "Do you have the poison in hand?"

"It was used up during the test."

Rodney sneered. "A convenient story. There was no poison."

"There is, or was. And I'll prove it, somehow."

The king rubbed at his beard. "Very well. Continue your investigation, Miss Storm. You have the royal permission to search where you will for this theoretical poison. We shall come to the truth of the matter. No, Captain Rodney. We have spoken."

"Does his Highness wish this humble servant to assist Miss Storm?" Pepe asked.

The king blinked at him. "You?"

"He's been very helpful," I added. "He gave me a tour of the games."

"Did he, now? As you wish." The king waved a hand.

Quill tugged at my sleeve. "Time to leave."

I backed out of the tent. Tricky started to follow me, a question in her dark eyes.

"Captain Tricky, a moment of your time," the king called out. "You too, Rodney. We need to discuss the burial arrangements. The funeral's in a matter of hours."

Pepe slipped out and joined us. The tent flap closed in front of Tricky's frown.

"That was some fancy sleuth work, Miss Storm," Pepe said. "Congratulations are in order."

"I suppose."

"Who do you need to visit first? I'm sure you have a few suspects in mind."

"Yes, but I doubt any of them will be happy with me boarding their ship."

Pepe smiled. "You leave that to me. I'll find some excuse to take you on board. You can look around while I distract the crew."

"Pepe! I need you in here at once," the king shouted.

"Duty calls." He bowed, then hurried back into the tent.

"He's rather helpful," I said.

"Don't trust the pirate who offers help," Quill's voice rumbled close to my ear. "They always want somethin'."

"You're helping me."

"Aye, but we're on the same crew. Besides, who says I don't want somethin'?"

"I can tell you what he wants," Pooky said.

"No, thanks. Shall we?"

I followed Quill down the beach. But something itched at the back of my neck, as if someone was sneaking up behind me with a club. The image was so persistent, I looked over my shoulder.

A figure retreated into the king's tent, and the flap fell back into place with a sharp *snap*.

Chapter Twenty-One

I'D NEVER BEEN to a funeral before — witches live long and prosper — so I wasn't sure what to expect. Especially since this was a pirate funeral.

"Will they toss his body overboard?" I asked Quill, who seemed not only knowledgeable in the pirate way, but more than willing to share what he knew.

"Only if he died out at sea. We pirates prefer land burials whenever possible."

"It really shouldn't matter," Pooky said as we joined the funeral procession filing across the beach. "The body's either devoured by little fish or by little worms."

"How touching," I said, stepping out of line to see the front of the crowd. Sweetie's body was wrapped in a hammock. "Why's he in a hammock?"

Scotty caught up to us as Quill answered, "Sailors're always buried in their hammock."

"I'm surprised he slept in one. As an officer, wouldn't he have his own room?"

"You mean cabin, aye." Scotty nodded. "He did, and I won this wager."

"You organized wagers for the funeral?"

Scotty jabbed a thumb over his shoulder at a few desolate-looking men. "Some of 'em been thinkin' Rodney'd make him a coffin. But I figured how Rodney thinks. Why waste the time and wood when every pirate keeps his hammock for this very occasion?"

"It's a mystery," I said.

Tricky snorted. "No. This is the pirate way."

Scotty and Quill nodded somberly. "Aye. The pirate way."

A few pirates had already dug a hole at the edge of the beach, close to the jungle. Brownbeard the Barbaric stood in place of a priest, standing by himself at the head of the grave. Everyone else gathered around, shuffling for a position closest to the hole.

I preferred to stay back. The sand wasn't stable, and I had no intention of tumbling into the grave along with Sweetie. I might never get out.

"Horrendous brethren of the pirate guild," the king intoned. "We submit to his final resting place Samuel Sweetie McFarson."

The crowd parted, and four of Sweetie's crewmates lined up on either side of the grave, the sewn-up hammock in hand.

"They don't look particularly upset," I whispered.

"Can't blame 'em," Quill said.

Scotty grinned. "Truth is, this was goin' to happen sooner or later."

Nearby pirates nodded but kept quiet when the king scowled.

"As a pirate, Sweetie wasn't particularly distinguished or good at his job. But he was one of us. And so we gather here today to respectfully toss his mortal remains into the ground and send him on his way."

"Hurrah!"

"Goodness, are all funerals like this?" I whispered.

"Ahh, no," Scotty said. "For them we like, we have a marchin' band and a huge keg of somethin' good. Why couldn't the murderer give us that much!"

Two pirates started shoveling sand into the grave. Tricky and Brownbeard were quietly consulting together. I had to remind myself that she was as much a suspect as anyone else.

"How're the election rankings for the king, Scotty?"

He grinned. "Oh, I see. So now you want to get in on the action?"

"No, I—"

"There's still time to place a wager, lass. Pirate elections're always unpredictable and volatile."

"I'm sure, but—"

"And not always peaceful, mind you. But always good fun. So who do you want to back?" He pulled out a small notebook.

"Actually, I just want to know who's ahead in the running."

"Rodney definitely slipped when one o' his own crewmembers died. Sloppy business, really. A good cap'n takes care of his crew, 'specially during an election. And 'specially when he's a frontrunner. But not anymore."

I gestured for him to hurry up. The sound of sand slapping against the canvas hammock reminded me we were at a funeral.

"The incumbent Brownbeard looked like a surefire winner at the start of it all, but he too has taken a beating in the rankings."

I studied Rodney, then Brownbeard. Rodney was chatting with Terrence Winks Wimble. The new quartermaster caught me looking at him and attempted to wink at me. It looked like his whole face was convulsing.

"Winks put his name into the ring as well," I murmured.

"That he did. Surprise contender, and not doin' too badly now that the two frontrunners have slipped in the race. Not bad at all."

I skipped over the king, and my gaze settled on Stinker, the pirate who found Sweetie. "And what about Stinker?"

Scotty snorted. "What about him? He's not even a candidate. Why?"

"Nothing. Anyone else?"

"Aye, a fair number. But the lot of 'em are so far back, they're not even worth mentionin'. Most of 'em put their names up for fun, not expecting or even wantin' the position. It comes with some degree of responsibility, you know. Heavy weighs the crown, as they say."

"Indeed."

More sand cascaded into the grave. The edges began to crumble, and pirates pushed against us to get away.

Scotty put away his notebook. "We might see an upset in the natural order. I've been managin' the wagers at these parlays for years now, and I've never seen the likes. I first thought the election was between Rodney and Brown-beard. Now, it's between Winks and Pepe."

I looked across the grave at Pepe. He was standing to one side of the king, his head bowed, hands clasped. "At least he's taking the funeral seriously."

"Don't know why. No one else is. Oi, you placed your bet, Stinker?" Scotty moved away, working the crowd, picking up a few more bets.

While there wasn't a marching band, the whole scene felt more fiesta than funeral.

"Are all human funerals like this?" I muttered.

"I wouldn't know," Pooky said and curled up on my feet. "Cats don't bother with such activities."

Once the sand had fully covered the grave, someone stuck a piece of wood at one end. Words were carved into it. "Here is Sweetie. He died as he lived."

"What's that supposed to mean?"

Pooky didn't bother answering, which was probably the best answer of all.

"Right." The pirate king slapped his hands, calling the crowd to attention. "Now that we've dispensed with the body, we'll be holding an auction for Sweetie's items."

"I thought the new quartermaster inherited them?" I didn't realize I'd spoken so loudly until several people turned to stare at me. I shrunk back, bumping against Quill's arm.

"I don't want anythin' of his," Winks said. "I'm not a big fan of his... um... style."

"Too sweet fer a self-respectin' pirate," someone else shouted and laughed.

Others joined in. Before long, laughter turned to singing. They loudly sang one of their favorites, the one about the misadventures of a sailor lost at sea. I stopped listening once they reached the chorus involving cannibalism and the importance of cooking your meat.

I turned to Quill. "I suppose we should set up my camp."

The pirate king must've had excellent hearing, for he said, "Not so fast, Miss Storm. Have you had sufficient time to analyze your evidence?"

"Not quite," I said. "But I'm working on it."

He frowned. "I suggest you work faster. The election is tomorrow night. The moment the sun touches the horizon, the pirates vote. And if we haven't solved the murder by then, I don't know if I'll be able to protect you." He strode past me, hand on his sword pummel, eyes straight ahead.

Chapter Twenty-Two

TRICKY MET with me to go over the night's plan. "Remind me what you're going to do here," she demanded.

"Sneak into all the tents, look for a pink, poisonous flower, and try not to get caught."

"Sounds good. Especially the *not getting caught* part."

I hesitated. "You told your crew they weren't allowed to spend the night on the beach. Too dangerous, you said."

"Aye. It is, but you aren't crew. So off you go."

"How reassuring."

Quill cleared his throat.

"Yes, Quill?" Tricky asked. "You catching a cold?"

"Permission to camp next to Miss Storm. For her safety, and all."

"How noble." Tricky puffed on her pipe, then nodded. "Very well. Don't get caught or killed or anything equally inconvenient. I have enough on my plate. Replacing a quartermaster isn't on the agenda."

Quill grinned. "This'll be fun."

His enthusiasm perked up my spirits. That lasted until

we started setting up our camp in a quiet corner of the beach at the edge of the jungle.

I held up a string which had seen better days in a previous century. "Are you sure these will hold?"

"Aye, without a doubt, miss." Quill tugged on a line and tied it around a tree. "You'll be snug as a bug in a rug."

"Is he comparing you to the bug or the rug?" Pooky asked.

I forced a smile. "As delightful as the image is of an insect inside a carpet, I'd rather be snug in a bed."

Quill winked, oblivious to my discomfort. "That you'll be. And if you need anythin', I'll be right next door." He patted the canvas he'd set up alongside my small tent.

"I feel better already."

"Aye, as do I."

I bit off my retort. Two tiny lights blinked from a nearby bush, snagging my attention. I peered closer. "How charming. Fireflies."

"Fireflies, here?" Quill shuffled closer and brandished a sword at the bush.

"That's hardly necessary. They don't bite."

"Not the normal kind, no. But you see fireflies this far south, take care. Them's not fireflies."

"Then what? Glowing mosquitos?"

"Aye, somethin' like that."

"Hmm. Shall we?"

We joined the pirates around the bonfire for a singa-long. I declined to sing. The lyrics centered around the pirate's life, which — according to the malcontent who wrote the songs — involved risking life and limb to steal gold, then bury it on an island no one would ever be able to find.

"It sounds rather pointless," I confided in Quill.

He paused in the middle of a chorus about a giant squid dragging a pirate ship down to a watery grave. "Not to worry. Us modern-day pirates don't bother buryin' treasure. We split it up fair-like."

"How evolved of you."

"Aye. We give a quarter to the captain, a small percentage to the king, a third to the officers—"

"A third each, or a third split among the officers?"

"Each... I think. And the rest is shared among the crew."

"I see. And those numbers add up, do they?"

He shrugged. "Close enough."

"Don't you think it's wrong to destroy other people's livelihoods for your own gain?"

"Oi, Miss Storm. We don't destroy other ships. We're pirates, not vandalizers."

"The word is vandals, not vandalizers."

He blinked a few times, then joined in the singalong for the rousing conclusion to the epic battle of *Captain Lucky and the Ridiculously Giant but Absolutely Real Squid*.

The pirate king interrupted the carousing to give announcements for the next day's events, including a few changes to the agenda. "We won't be playing Hangman this year."

The crowd erupted in a series of boos.

He held up a hand. "I know. It's disappointing."

"Why not?" Quill shouted.

"On account of last year's unfortunate demise of a pirate who was a tad too enthusiastic when he tied the knot around his neck. You know of whom I speak."

Pirates nodded and muttered to each other.

"And anyone who knows how to stitch up a toe, Stinker'd be grateful."

"He means stitch up a cut, right?" I whispered to Quill.

He chuckled. "Oh, no. He means stitch a toe. Stinker lost another one in the sword-tossing competition."

"Another… Why do you have these competitions?"

"To prove our pirate mettle."

Brownbeard dismissed us, wishing us a good night's sleep that didn't involve knives, swords, pistols or poison. A few pirates tittered at the mention of poison and glanced over at me.

"I gather everyone knows I found poison in the tea?" I asked.

Quill nodded. "Aye, o' course. No secrets among pirates, we say."

"If there are no secrets, then why don't we know who the murderer is?"

"There's always a few rotten limbs in every barrel, Miss Storm."

"You mean bad apples."

"What?"

"The expression is a few bad apples… never mind. Let's get back to our camp and wait for everyone to settle down."

We entered our respective tents, snuffed out our candles, and pretended to sleep. In Quill's case, the pretense didn't last very long. His soft snores trickled through the canvas like a persistent mosquito.

"What shall we do now?" Pooky asked, curling up in my lap.

"Not fall asleep before everyone else does."

"Good. Then you have time to listen to my tale of woe."

"Time, but no interest."

"It's a very interesting story."

"I'm sure it isn't."

"I was but a wee lad when my mother's noble spirit

departed her mortal form and winged its way to the heaven reserved for all gods and godlike creatures. In other words, cats."

I yawned and lay down. This was going to take some time. Pirates were still singing their utterly inappropriate songs as they staggered back to their tents or rowboats.

"Left to my own devices, I set off to make my fortune in the grand metropolis of Catnip City."

"There's no such place."

Pooky sighed loudly. "In human tongue, it's referred to as London."

"Ah. Of course."

"Please stop interrupting me. It's terribly rude. I arrived in Catnip… *London* with only what I was wearing."

"Your fur."

"Again. The interruptions. At this rate, it'll take all night and into tomorrow to finish."

"My apologies. Continue."

"As I was saying, I explored the streets of London and quickly determined it was a dangerous and unkind place for a young cat on his own. Even a cat as magnificent as myself." He paused. "You can applaud."

I tapped my hands together a couple of times.

"Thank you. Having thus discovered my dilemma, I decided to procure a set of boots—"

"Boots?"

"That's what I said. Four white leather boots. You've seen the imprint they left on my limbs. No matter how I groom, the white marks on my paws remain. But it was worth the sacrifice of my beautiful all-black fur. For upon fitting myself with four leather boots, I became quite famous as a hunter for hire."

"What did you hunt?"

"Ogres, mostly."

"Really. You hunted ogres. While wearing boots."

"*Leather* boots. And yes. I was a fearsome hunter. Shall I describe one of my more famous exploits?"

"Hmm." My eyes slid closed.

"Excellent decision. So there I was, in the Forest of Gingerbread. It was a place famous for its gingerbread infrastructure and ogres."

Pooky's voice faded as I fell into a light slumber. A bright pink flower filled my vision. The horrendously smelly *Decaying Corpses*, the poisonous sap of which had been used to murder Sweetie.

The dream tugged on my memories. I was back in Sweetie's tent, brushing crystals off of the table. Sugar crystals laced with poison. Sweetie sat across from me, smiling and encouraging me to put sugar in my tea. Then...

I jerked awake.

"And that's how I met Queen Victoria," Pooky said, his head tucked under my chin. "Once I shared my story with her through a translator, she naturally knighted me."

I pushed Pooky off my chest. "What time is it?"

"Time does flit by when listening to a story as riveting as mine. But I don't keep track of such trivial details."

I sat up. The beach was quiet apart from small waves lapping over sand. "Quill, wake up."

He snorted and rolled over, his face pressing up against my tarp. "Aye, my big toe is a handsome specimen," he mumbled in his sleep.

"How dare he fall asleep," Pooky said. "You should've translated everything for him—"

"Shh."

"You don't shush a knight of Her Majesty's Empire."

I tugged my blanket up to my chin. "Did you hear that?"

"You mean the verbal rudeness directed at me? It was hard to miss."

Sand rustled outside my tent.

"Quill?" I whispered, even though I knew it wasn't him.

The flap at the front of my tent shifted aside, revealing a human-shaped silhouette holding a knife.

Chapter Twenty-Three

THE SILHOUETTE at the entrance of my tent stooped over, a knife held before it.

I didn't think. I didn't have time to pull out my vial of freshwater, concoct a spell and toss it at the intruder. If I had, I would've blinded him with spiderweb netting, or turned his knife into mush.

Or at the very least, I could've performed a spell I already knew, such as the power punch. A nifty one to use when confronted with an unknown pirate holding a dagger.

Instead, I snatched up the closest thing, which happened to be a cat. Ignoring Pooky's squeal of protest, I tossed him at the man's head.

"Argh!"

The pirate screamed, the cat howled, and I thumped Quill's face through the canvas. He rolled the other way and snored louder.

"Unbelievable. Who's protecting whom?" I tugged at the bottom of the canvas, searching for an escape route.

Quill had pegged my tent down firmly in order to

prevent any creepy crawlies from sneaking underneath. A pity he hadn't done the same for the front flap. A corner of the tent loosened under my efforts, and I yanked it open. Then I crawled through the small opening, my fingers digging into the sand.

Something snapped in the darkness, and the tent collapsed on my legs.

It was a good thing Grand Dame Puddlewick couldn't see me now. She'd be horrified. Upholding the honor and dignity of the Puddlewick family name was always front and center for her. And here I was, quite literally dragging myself through damp sand.

"I'm not happy about this!" Pooky wailed. "Weren't you listening to my story? I've had enough trauma in my life!"

"Sorry!" I staggered to a standing position and made one last attempt to wake Quill with no success.

A second later, a small shadow clawed at my pantaloons. "You owe me. Forever. Countless dishes of full-fat cream."

I gathered Pooky in my arms and sprinted away from the tent.

"Did you hear me?"

"Absolutely. Less talking, more running," I huffed.

"Good idea, because that intruder who damaged one of my claws? He's coming after us."

I ran in the only direction available to me: the jungle. It wasn't the smartest move in hindsight. Then again, camping on a beach full of pirates after the pirate king had revealed my discovery wasn't exactly high on the list of clever things to do.

"Get back here," a gruff voice bellowed.

"That doesn't sound like anyone we know," Pooky said.

"This is my stop." He wiggled out of my arms and scrambled up a tree.

I kept running, stumbling in the dark. Pooky was right. The voice sounded strange, almost forced. As if the person was disguising his voice in case he couldn't catch me.

"Climb a tree!" Pooky shouted.

It was a good idea, but I had none of the tools required to do so. My nails were short, and my stature didn't allow me to reach one of the lower branches. So I kept running, searching for a place I could hide or a way back to the beach. If I could just reach Quill, he'd buy me some time to fix a spell. That is, if he woke up.

"You're running in circles," Pooky said.

I glanced up. He was sitting on a branch, cleaning his paws.

Twigs snapped behind me as my pursuer crashed through the undergrowth.

"The beach must be this way, then," I decided and continued running.

"You're still going the wrong way," Pooky said. "And in circles. This is fun. We should do this more often."

I jogged back toward his tree and crouched in the shadows. I held my breath, listening for the intruder while trying to get my bearings. The jungle was quiet apart from insect tweets, a lonely bird's hooting, and the strangled cry of a distant creature. Either the man had given up, or was listening for me.

A small creature scuttled in the branches above me.

"Is that you, Pooky?"

"Wrong tree. I'm over here."

I glanced over at the other tree. "How can you see so well?"

"Don't you wish you were a cat now?"

I pulled out my vial of water and tipped a few drops in the palm of my hand.

"This should be entertaining," Pooky said.

"Hush. Go over there and make some noise." I gestured deeper into the jungle.

"No, thank you. There's a large, carnivorous creature living around here."

"Now you tell me?"

"The topic never came up before, quite honestly. I didn't think it was too important."

"That there's a large carnivore living near where I'm sleeping?"

"Humph. Since you put it that way, I can see why you might want me to tell you about it."

"Unbelievable."

Leaves rustled off to my right. I spun around, squatting behind a bush. I lowered a branch and stared. It was Terrence Wink Wimble. What was he doing here?

Winks held up a thick candle, frowning as he continued deeper into the jungle. I was tempted to follow him, until I remembered I was alone and unarmed. Well, not entirely unarmed. I did have a few decent spells up my sleeve. I stood and was about to go after Winks when Pooky hissed.

"What is it?"

"Something's coming this way."

I frowned, wondering how many of us were running around the jungle in the middle of the night.

"It could be that giant carnivore I mentioned earlier."

I closed my eyes, scrambling for a spell that might help. Night vision? Useful, but it wouldn't save me from whoever or whatever was coming for me.

Power punch? Always a classic. One could never go wrong with the ability to knock some sense into an offensive creature. Man or carnivore, it made no difference.

"Power punch it is." I began to chant. *"Double, double toil and trouble. Fire burn and cauldron bubble. Power of rock and strength of might. Let me win this coming fight."*

The water glittered with blue light, then sunk into my palm. My skin tingled, and my hand started to throb.

"Is your hand supposed to do that?" Pooky asked.

"I'm not sure."

"You've used the spell before, haven't you?"

"No. Not exactly."

"That doesn't sound reassuring."

"I saw Grand Dame Puddlewick demonstrate it before."

"Your hand looks like it's blowing up."

I held up my arm. My hand was now swollen to twice its normal size, and still growing.

"Great. How am I going to hide this?"

"Never mind hiding it. How about you use it on whatever is coming toward you right now?"

"Again, a little bit more warning." I pressed my back against the tree trunk and peered around.

Leaves crackled as someone or something stalked toward me.

"I'm armed," I said, hoping the waver in my voice wasn't obvious.

"Miss Storm?"

I exhaled loudly. "Oh, it's just you, Pepe."

"Just me?" He stepped closer, holding up a lantern. "That's not exactly how I want to be greeted."

"I'm so sorry."

He glanced at my hand, then gasped. "Your hand! What happened?"

"A bee sting."

"A bee sting did that to you?"

"Yes. That's what happened. A bee. Did you happen to see Winks?"

Pepe rubbed his chin. "Can't say I have. What're you doing out here, Miss Storm?"

"An excellent question," Pooky said. "It started when she fell asleep during the recitation of my life story—"

"I thought I heard someone outside my tent," I said.

"Heavens. Did you see what he looks like?"

"Again with the rudeness," Pooky muttered. "She saw nothing. But I definitely smelled something."

"Sadly not," I said, trying to keep track of the conversation. Pooky wasn't making it easy.

Pepe took a step closer. "It's not safe out here, Miss Storm—"

"Miss Storm!" Quill shouted.

Pepe and I both startled and turned toward the sound of Quill's voice.

"Over here, Quill," I called out.

Quill barged through a thick web of vines, breaking them with the sheer force of his momentum. "It's not safe to be roamin' 'round at night. 'Specially out here on your own."

"My heroes." But I stopped paying attention to Quill's lecture. Something more interesting had caught my attention: the soft pink petals of a *Decaying Corpses* flower growing under the roots of a nearby tree.

Chapter Twenty-Four

"WE SHOULD GO BACK to the ship." Quill paused and yawned. "Or back to sleep."

I sat hunched over at the entrance to my semi-collapsed tent, blanket wrapped around my shoulders. "How can you sleep at a time like this?"

Quill winked and grinned. "Easy as catchin' stranded fish."

"I fail to see how fishing and sleeping are connected."

"They're both easy."

Pooky curled up on my lap. "I concur with the pirate. I need a nap after all that excitement."

I glanced toward Sweetie's tent. "*Decaying Corpses* is here."

"I told Captain Rodney he should bury Sweetie sooner than later."

"Not *that* corpse. I mean the poisonous flower is native to this island. It's in the jungle."

"So?"

I turned in the other direction. Pepe had returned to he king's camp after ensuring I was safely back at mine.

"It means someone knows enough about botany to recognize it as poisonous. And they know how to prepare the flower's sap correctly. These are not basic skills."

Quill's jaw almost unhinged with his next yawn. "Huh. You want to sleep on the ship or in your tent? I'm okay with either."

"Whoever murdered Sweetie is an amateur botanist. And a decent one, at that."

"I'm thinkin' we stay here. It's late. Kind o' cold. And no one's goin' to bother you again. Know why? 'Cause I'm sleepin' in the tent with you."

"You're right. We need to investigate all the tents while everyone's fast asleep."

Quill scrubbed his face. "That's not what I said."

"But it's what you meant. Because of course we're not going to sleep until we find proof. And you're certainly not going to sleep in my tent while I'm in it."

Quill shrugged. "Worth a shot."

"You're incorrigible."

"That's not true. I can be corrupted. Anytime."

"That's not what… Forget it. How many pirates do you think are camped on this beach?"

Quill looked around. "Apart from *The Pink Pearl*, most o' the crews are here. Only a few're guardin' the ships."

"So how many?"

"A lot?"

"I suspect there must be more than a hundred, although most aren't in tents."

Pooky sniffed. "I'm not sure he can count that high."

I bit my lower lip to prevent laughter from spurting out. I studied the beach. The rank and file of pirates didn't have a tent, nor did they need one. They either slept in hammocks, or in simple lean-to's, partially open to the elements. There was no place to hide evidence in such shelters.

I turned my attention to the few tents set up in various clusters. Officers, older pirates, and captains.

"We shall have to assume the murderer is here," I said. "Boarding the ships might be problematic, even with a skeleton crew."

"You think the murderer'll keep proof here, in an unsecured location?" Quill asked.

He had a point.

"And you're goin' to sneak into all o' these tents?"

My shoulders sagged.

"And what if one of 'em wakes up and finds you in there? Talk about corruptible."

"Then what do you suggest?"

"Sleep. If you still want, we explore the tents tomorrow durin' the grand finale."

"That's actually not a terrible idea."

Quill chuckled. "I've been known to have a not-terrible idea on occasion. So, same tent?"

I crawled back into my tent. "You can sleep in front of my doorway."

"I'll take what I can."

I was awoken at first light by a blaring horn.

Pooky pawed at my face. "What's wrong with these humans?"

"I don't know," I muttered. "There's no need to wake up *everyone* if they want to be a bird."

"It's the sunrise race," Quill said from the other side of the tent flap. "Best day o' the year."

"That doesn't say much for the rest of your life."

The tent flap moved aside, revealing an expression far too cheerful for this time in the morning. "You've never seen pirates race, then. It's a sight to behold."

"I'm sure it is. But we'll be doing something else."

"We will? Tell me more."

I kicked the flap shut before he could make any inappropriate comments to match his smug smile.

Breakfast was a hurried affair. My stomach didn't approve. Neither did the cat.

"Humans. Always rushing back and forth. You'd think they actually had something important they were doing." Pooky wrinkled his nose. "There's *nothing* important about any of this."

I kept quiet. Several pirates had already caught me talking to the cat. I didn't need to add to the suspicion that I was a tad odd in the head.

The race seemed simple enough. The pirate ships all lined up at the entrance of the cove. When the pistol fired, the ships sailed out to some point, collected a flag that was tied to a buoy, and sailed back.

"I believe you're right," I whispered. "It is rather pointless."

Pooky licked a paw. "You're finally understanding the wisdom of the cat."

As per our hastily created plan, I hid in my tent. Quill reluctantly joined Tricky on her ship. It would raise eyebrows and more than a few questions if the ship was missing its quartermaster.

"We don't need that big oaf, anyway. I'll take care of our plan," Pooky reassured me, then promptly fell asleep.

The ships jostled around the cove until they were lined up in some semblance of order. *The Dolphin's Kiss* was also in the race. The pirate king strutted across his deck, giving unnecessary orders to his crew.

"Come on," I muttered. I didn't know how much time they'd spend racing, or if I had time to visit every tent. It was going to be tight, even though the number of tents were far less than the number of pirates.

A pistol exploded across the silence. Loud cheers echoed across the cove as the ships began to move to the open ocean.

"Wake up, Pooky. Now's our chance."

"Our chance to sleep in," Pooky mumbled.

"I mean it."

"So do I. Admit you can't manage without me, and I'll come."

"I'm going."

"Okay, you don't need to beg." He stretched and followed me outside.

I decided to check quartermaster Winks' tent first, since he had the most to gain from Sweetie's demise. As none of the tents were labeled, I entered each one in Rodney's camp. They were surprisingly bare, with only a mattress, a blanket and a few items of clothes stored in small chests. I rummaged through them, then popped into the next tent. By the fifth tent, I was puffing.

"Are we done yet?" Pooky asked from his perch on a nearby rock. His eyes were closed, and he faced the sun.

"No, and I'd appreciate your assistance."

"I'm sure you would."

I entered the next tent. Again it was sparse, and I half-heartedly rummaged through a pile of clothing. It was a waste of time, I decided.

Of course no one kept evidence in their tent. Quill was right. Pooky was right. It was all useless. I could be sitting on *The Pink Pearl*, sipping tea and enjoying the sea breeze instead of rummaging through stuffy, smelly tents that were growing progressively warmer by every minute. I might as well return to my tent and follow Pooky's example.

My fingers grazed across a small packet. I picked it up and smiled. "Hello, evidence."

In my hand was a small, precious packet of sugar. I turned it over. I recognized the seal.

This was Sweetie's stolen sugar.

Chapter Twenty-Five

THE PINK PEARL won the race.

The shouting and *Hurrahs* were loud enough that I was grateful not to be on deck. I valued my hearing.

The Dolphin's Kiss was right behind her, but far enough back that there was no mistaking which ship crossed the finish first. That didn't stop Brownbeard the Barbaric from protesting the results.

"I won," he declared when the captains and a lot of the crew had reached the beach. "You only think you did because of the angle. But I actually crossed the finish first."

Tricky clamped her teeth around her pipe so hard, I expected something to crack. "Your Royal Ugliness, you always were a sore loser. I won, fair and square."

"You mean unfair and round."

"Even better. Pay up."

To my surprise, Rodney backed Tricky. "It's true, your Barbaric Highness. I tied with you for second place—"

"You did not!"

Winks nodded. "Aye. We did, at that. Second place."

"So I saw it clear as the wart on Scribbles' nose,"

Rodney continued, ignoring his quartermaster. "She won. Totally unfair, cheated the entire way—"

"Thank you," Tricky said.

"And I wouldn't be surprised if she damaged your ship at some point."

"I have my limits. Hurting a ship crosses the line," Tricky said and glared at Rodney.

Rodney smirked. "Such a pity Tricky didn't put her name up in this year's kingly election. Pirates vote for winners. She might've won the crown tonight. We've never had a pirate queen before."

"We will if you win the vote," Tricky drawled.

"You, there. Stowaway." The pirate king waved at me.

"Tell them you were sick," Pooky advised. "Or sleeping. Yes, that would be the best excuse. You were sleeping, and didn't see anything."

"You were on the beach. Who won?" Brownbeard demanded.

Everyone turned their attention on me.

"Say nothing. Say… nothing," Pooky mumbled by my side.

Tricky glowered at me. The pirate king scowled, and Rodney smirked, no doubt anticipating more entertainment at my expense.

"The thing is, your Barbaric Highness, *The Pink Pearl* did seem to arrive first," I said, my voice wavering at the end.

"Hurrah!"

Tricky smiled around her pipe stem.

"And you, Miss Storm? I'm betrayed on all sides." Brownbeard shook his head, the picture of desolation.

"Sir, whose tent is that?" I pointed at the tent in which I'd found Sweetie's sugar.

"It's mine, miss," Winks said and stepped forward. "There be a problem?"

"Can you explain how this came to be in your tent?" I held up the packet with Sweetie's seal clearly visible.

Rodney gasped. "You?"

Winks wasn't quite as quick in picking up on the implication. "That's not my sugar."

The pirate king grinned, probably grateful for a chance to divert attention from his loss. "No, it's not. That packet belonged to Sweetie. So how did it end up in your tent?"

"Blasted barnacles," Stubbs grumbled. "Khalid really is innocent, him an' his blasted unibrow."

"What does his eyebrow have to do with it?" I asked.

"Can't trust no man with one eyebrow," Stubbs said.

Khalif scowled, then started to laugh. "This proves Khalid's innocent, and Winks is the culprit!"

"Hurrah!" *The Pink Pearl* crew shouted.

Winks backed away, hands up. "No. I don't know how that packet got in my tent. I swear. I didn't like Sweetie. No one really did. But I didn't hurt him. Or kill him."

Tricky scoffed. "You planted that knife to blame one of my crewmembers. Your Royal Barbaricness, I insist you release my crewmember immediately, and imprison this scoundrel for murder during the sacred pirate parlay."

"How could you?" Rodney asked, his expression like a child who just learned his favorite fairytale wasn't true.

"I didn't, I swear, captain."

Rodney's expression hardened. "I promoted you from part-time quartermaster to full-time quartermaster. And this is how you repay me? At least you could've told me. You know how embarrassing it is to find out in public that my second-in-command killed my former second-in-command?"

"You're upset about learning the truth in public, rather

than learning one of your crew murdered another crewmember?" I asked.

"Of course. Sweetie was the worst quartermaster ever. Why do you think I had to appoint a part-time quartermaster?"

Scribbles stepped forward and unrolled a scroll. "Let it be recorded. Khalid of *The Pink Pearl* is hereby declared innocent of this specific crime—"

"Hurrah!"

"And Terrence Winks Wimble will spend the remainder of the pirate parlay in the pit, after which he shall face justice. So it has been decreed."

No one cheered at the second announcement. Two of the king's crew escorted a loudly protesting Winks to the pit.

"Rodney's position's sure to fall in the charts after this," Scotty muttered. "'Specially since he didn't win the race. And based on current stuff, Pepe Le Pirate's ranking'll drift to the top. Not bad."

Stubbs softly cursed.

"Good job," the king gruffly commented as he passed me. "Just in time for the grand feast."

Tricky tipped her head toward me, puffed out a ring of smoke, and followed the king.

"Congratulations," Pooky said. "Now about that nap."

"This doesn't feel right," I said.

Pooky flicked sand off a paw. "Of course not. We're stuck on Treasure Island, which has no treasure, with several boatloads of pirates, next to a jungle filled with poisonous flowers and a giant carnivore. This is precisely why we must return to the ship and take a long nap, preferably one lasting until we leave this place."

Khalif jogged up to me, wrapped me in his arms and squeezed tightly. "Thank you, Miss Storm. I'm forever in your debt. May my life be a sacrifice. You are the beat in my heart, the air in my lungs—"

"Speaking of air." I wiggled out of his enthusiastic grasp. "A simple thank you will suffice, please."

"I thank you from the depths of my beating heart, from the bottom of my wretched soul. Whatever you ask, it shall be given. A thousand blessings upon you. May you live to have many sons—"

"Slow down there, pirate," Pooky said and swatted at his leg. "How many sons are we talking about?"

"Thank you for the dubious blessings," I said. "Make me a pot of tea, and we'll call it even."

Khalif straightened. "My brother's life is worth far more than one pot of tea."

"Are you sure?" Pooky asked.

"I'm sure it is," I said. "But all I wish at this moment is a pot of tea and some silence."

Khalif bowed, stepped backward a few paces, then ran to the fire pit.

"You really should've asked for more," Pooky said. "A lifetime of tea in bed. Or better yet, cream! One can never have too much cream. You really need to work on your imagination."

"Lack of imagination isn't the problem. Winks isn't the botanist type."

"Sure he is."

"Remember when he said he was allergic to you?"

Pooky shuddered. "I'm blocking that trauma from my memory."

"He also mentioned being allergic to all tropical vegetation."

"So what? Maybe he held his breath when he made the poison. Or wore a mask. Case closed. Can I go now? Your mattress is calling my name. Can you hear it calling? *Pooky.*

Pooky, come sleep on me, you beautiful cat. Besides, you need your beauty sleep."

I crouched in front of Pooky. "I think someone's trying to frame Winks."

"Why do that? He'd make a terrible painting."

"Not that sort of frame. The election's tonight, and Rodney's one of the candidates."

"Good for him."

"But the pirates will think ill of him, now that his quartermaster has been accused of murder."

"Why? They're pirates. They love murder and mayhem."

"Not as much as most people think, and certainly not around a captain or their king. It shows lack of effective leadership. Pirates look for a strong commander they respect. Who's going to respect a captain who can't protect or manage his crew?"

Pooky yawned. "And your point is…"

"Winks isn't the murderer. Which means whoever killed Sweetie is still on the loose."

Chapter Twenty-Six

"WE HAVE to find the real murderer before the elections tonight," I said as I hurried to find Quill.

"I don't see why you care so much," Pooky said as he waddled by my side. "You've solved the murder — twice — proved you're useful to the captain, and probably won't have to walk the plank. The jury's still out on the whole joining the chief's harem. But that won't be such a bad life. It's certainly better than sinking to the bottom of the ocean."

"Don't you care there's a murderer out there?"

"There are murderers everywhere. We're surrounded by them. These are pirates! Of course they're going to murder each other."

I shook my head. Pooky was wrong. Sure, the pirates liked to talk a big story, about pillaging and taking over other ships. But the pirates also had a code — the Pirate Codex. Each ship had its own particular version. From what I'd witnessed, the pirates took it seriously and adhered to all the principles within it.

"Quill, I need you."

Quill immediately broke away from his conversation with Stubbs and strutted toward me. "Words I've been longin' to hear!"

"Do you want me to scratch him?" Pooky looked up at me. "I'll do it. Gladly. And I won't charge you for it. Give me the word. Or a nod. Nod at me, and I'll—"

I waved at the cat. "I believe the wrong man's in that pit."

Quill sobered up. "You're sure? It's quite somethin' to change your accusation. Winks might even challenge you to a duel for falsely accusing him o' murder."

"Oh. Well, I didn't technically accuse him. I merely said I found Sweetie's sugar in his tent. Everyone else jumped to the conclusion."

Quill winked. "You're a clever one, you are, Miss Storm. So who's the culprit, then?"

"I'm not sure. But I may know how to find out."

"Without using your magic?" Pooky asked.

"Does it involve a bit of mischief and mayhem?"

I shrugged. "Perhaps a bit, and we need to break into a ship or two."

Quill held out a fist and jerked it down. "Yes! Count me in, Miss Storm. And don't worry 'bout Winks. I'll deal with him if he dares challenge you."

"Our hero," Pooky muttered.

One of the final events for the pirate parlay was a feast held in the early evening. The twin brothers along with every other cook from all the ships had already started their preparations at the fire pit.

"And that's when we'll go," I said. "Everyone should be here on the beach, settling in for the farewell dinner. According to the agenda, it's the king's big event where he gives his speeches, indirectly or directly explains why everyone should vote for him, and then gives the floor to other candidates. It's very clever, really. People are far friendlier when they've been given a good feast."

Quill looked forlornly toward the fire pit where the cooks were busy at work. "So we're goin' to miss the meal?"

"I don't think so, but I can go by myself—"

"I won't hear o' it. There'll be a guard or two left on the ships. I can't have you goin' there by yourself, alone, defenseless."

Pooky hissed. "She has me."

"Very gallant of you, Quill," I said. "And we'll be back in time to eat. After all, we need to solve the murder *before* the elections, which occur during the feast."

"Please tell me you're *not* going to have offspring with this pirate," Pooky said. "There's only so much shock and trauma I can handle in one day."

I picked up Pooky and stroked him under the chin. "I suggest we go now, on the pretense that I need to change or something like that."

"Are you goin' to wear a dress?" Quill asked, his eyes widening.

"It's a pretense, Quill. I'm not really going to change."

"Oh. You really should, though. The feast's a formal thing."

"Please let me scratch out his eyes," Pooky pleaded.

"Perhaps. Shall we?" I walked toward one of *The Pink Pearl*'s rowboats.

"I now see why it's so complicated for humans to find an appropriate mate," Pooky said. "You don't have a lot of good options. You should try changing into a cat. I hear some witches are able to do that. You'd have so many better options that way. I myself could introduce you to a few of them."

"That cat sure is noisy," Quill said.

"But occasionally he does make some sense," I said, ignoring Quill's confused expression.

Nobody questioned our explanation. Nobody questioned us at all. A number of other pirates were going back and forth between the beach and the ships, bringing over supplies, or their finest clothes. I was curious what the king planned on wearing, especially since his normal attire was fancy already. But we might not see much of the feast unless we hurried.

"So what now?" Quill asked when we reached *The Pink Pearl.*

"We wait until most of the pirates are at the feast," I explained as we hurried toward the pantry. "Then we'll visit the other ships. While we're here, we can also take a look at the crew's quarters."

Quill stopped so abruptly, I turned to see what had happened.

"You're going to investigate your own crew?"

"They're not my…" I exhaled loudly. "Yes. Everyone is potentially a suspect."

He gawked. "You mean… you mean you suspect someone on our crew?"

"Not specifically, no. But we can't overlook the possibility. And besides, we're already here. So what's the problem?"

Quill choked, producing a gargling noise that sounded like, "Not our own crew!"

"I see I don't have to worry about you mating with him," Pooky said.

"I'm going to change. You should, too. That way, we don't have to lie about it."

"We just have to break into our own crew's quarters," Quill said in a dreary voice.

"Cheer up. I'm sure everyone here is perfectly innocent of this crime."

"That's the problem. I'm sure they are. Such a pity." He marched down to the main deck, shaking his head.

"Did you understand any of that?" Pooky asked.

"It's best we don't think too much on the matter. There're many things we don't understand."

Pooky snickered. "This is the pirate way."

I giggled. "Tricky does take it seriously, though."

"Humans. Can't live with them. Can't live with them."

Chapter Twenty-Seven

QUILL WAS RIGHT. He was also disappointed. When we inspected the quarters of *The Pink Pearl*'s crew, they all came out clean. Well, not exactly *clean*. But I couldn't find evidence connecting any of the crew to Sweetie's murder.

"Told you none o' them did it," Quill said and slumped down on a steamer trunk.

"Chin up. I'm sure your crewmembers are a villainous bunch. They simply missed this opportunity. There'll be others."

"You think so?"

"Absolutely."

Quill perked up. "You're right."

"Exactly. There's no point in dwelling on the past."

"Aye. Now what?"

I peered out the porthole. It was late in the afternoon, and most of the rowboats were now on the beach, along with the pirates. The bonfire was roaring, and what looked like an entire cow was being roasted over it.

"I believe it's time we did a bit of sleuthing."

"You mean skulking."

"No, I… I suppose so."

"Be still my heart," Quill murmured. "A woman who skulks is a fine woman indeed."

"Then you're going to love this." I pulled my lock pick set out of my pocket.

Quill thumped his hands over his heart. "You're a treasure among womenkind."

I curtsied.

"And you look fetchin' in a dress, Miss Storm. It suits you well."

"Thank you. Although I must say I prefer the pantaloons. They're far more practical for what we're about to do." I dared to lift up my skirt, revealing the pantaloons underneath.

"Aye, more practical, but not quite as charmin'."

I shrugged. I wasn't trying to impress him after all. I needed to solve this case properly for the third time, so I could go on with my plan to reach the New World and a new life.

We decided to first go to Rodney's ship, *The Red-Eyed Squid*. He was a contender in tonight's election for the throne and had the most to gain from embarrassing the current king. Then again, his quartermaster either being murdered or arrested didn't bode well for his prospects. But as it was the closest ship, we went there.

"Let me go first. Make sure we don't have unexpected company," Quill said and scurried up the rope ladder hanging off the side of *The Red-Eyed Squid*.

Minutes ticked by. I tugged at the starched, lacy collar around my neck. "I forgot how uncomfortable modern fashion is for women."

Pooky stared at me unblinkingly. "Another reason to become a cat. We don't wear clothes."

"Except when you wear boots."

"Naturally. But boots don't count."

"Miss Storm!"

I looked up. Quill waved at me.

"I suppose I'll have to accustom myself to the hardships of feminine Victorian fashion." I tucked Pooky into a small carry bag. "People on land won't be so appreciative of a woman wearing men's attire."

"If I didn't know better, it sounds like you might actually miss life on *The Pink Pearl*."

I snickered. "This is the pirate way."

"It is. At least they don't smell as bad as the London humans."

Quill helped me over the rail, and I hiked up my dress to give me more opportunity to run if the need arose.

"Has anyone ever told you how beautiful your ankles are?" Quill murmured as he led me toward the crew's quarters.

"That's kind and very forward of you. Shall we hurry this along? We have several other ships to investigate."

We descended the stairs. *The Red-Eyed Squid* had a similar setup to *The Pink Pearl*, except it was bigger. It also felt more elaborate, no doubt thanks to Rodney's ambitious nature. Tricky struck me as a person who was content without needing a constant stream of more possessions.

Most of the cabins were unlocked. The general quarters were a series of hammocks and bunkbeds for the sailor class. We found plenty of evidence of crime but none of it related to Sweetie. Similarly, the officers' cabins provided no clues or hints.

"Here must be the captain's quarters," Quill said as we reached the end of the hallway. He eased open a door.

The inside of Rodney's quarters looked like a museum. Artifacts from various cultures cluttered shelves and tabletops. His bed, while narrow, had a rich tapestry as a blanket.

Quill whistled. "Wee Rodney knows how to live it up."

I opened and closed the drawers of his writing desk, shuffling through papers and scrolls. "Nothing here. Check that cabinet."

"Nothin' too interesting here, either. Oh, wait. Spoke too soon, I did. Naughty Rodney." Quill removed a poster of an alluring woman wearing only her undergarments. "Ever seen one o' these, Miss Storm?"

I quickly averted my gaze. "No, and I'll thank you very much for not exposing my innocent eyes to such risqué images."

Pooky snorted as he curled up on the tapestry quilt. "Innocent? I think not. You were raised by Grand Dame Puddlewick. You know how to poison a person in half a dozen different ways."

I smiled. Pooky wasn't wrong. But Grand Dame Puddlewick also had her standards, as did I.

"Wee Rodney?" a squeaky voice called out.

Quill and I froze, staring at each other.

"Who's that?" Quill whispered.

"It sounds like his mother."

Quill nodded. "You're right. As usual. I should probably get used to that, shouldn't I?"

"Absolutely. Now stop talking."

Floorboards creaked as Mrs. Montoya approached her son's cabin. "Rodney? You there? I overslept. You promised ta wake me in time. Looks like everyone's already on the beach. Rodney?"

"Another great thing about being a cat is we're really small," Pooky said. "We can hide. We can become practically invisible. Watch and learn. *Invisible*."

"Good for you," I whispered and opened the door of the wardrobe in one corner. "Quill, quickly. In here."

Quill was a big fellow, tall and muscular. I didn't realize just how tall or how muscular he was until we crammed ourselves between Rodney's frilly jackets and elaborate suits. I eased the door shut just as Rodney's mom entered the cabin.

"Oh. I coulda sworn I heard… Hello, pussy. Where'd you come from?"

Pooky hissed.

"There, there. One o' me son's experiments, then?"

"Humph! I should say not. Unhand me, you brutish human."

"He left already, didn't he?" Mrs. Montoya sniffed. "Ungrateful child. That's whatcha get. Sacrifice me whole life. Work hard fer him, help him ta get promoted. You listenin' ta me, pussy? I did it all fer him, and this is me reward. Left here instead o' bein' out there for the great feast. You're a pretty little thing, though. Come along, then. I'm callin' you Spot."

"Help. Me!" Pooky meowed pitifully.

"And when Rodney comes back, I'll give him a piece of me mind, I will. Abandonin' me like this. You'd think he was embarrassed ta have me at the party. But I was the one who made him what he is. He forgets that. Don't worry, Spot. I'll remind him. In painful measure. Who was it that paved the way fer him ta become captain of *The Red-Eyed Squid*? Me. That's who."

She continued rambling as she drifted back down the hallway. I held my breath, trying not to wiggle. Quill's presence dominated the small space. And I couldn't help but notice how muscular his arm was, pressed up against me.

"I think we can go out now," I whispered.

"Really? Maybe we should wait a few minutes. It's quite cozy in here, isn't it, Miss Storm?"

I pushed open the wardrobe door and stumbled out. "You really are incorrigible."

"If you say so. Okay, next ship—"

Pooky's screech bounced down the hallway.

I sighed. "I can't leave Pooky here."

"I'll get you another cat."

"Tempting. But this cat is rather… special."

"If you say so. Here's the plan. I'll knock her out. You grab the cat."

"No! You're not going to attack a nice little old lady."

"Course not. I'm goin' to knock out Rodney's ma."

"That's who I meant."

"Oi! Have you met her? Sure, she's little. And old. But she definitely ain't nice."

I peered into the hallway. There was no sign of cat or old lady.

"Here's the plan," I said as we tiptoed down the hallway in the direction of the cat's hissing and Mrs. Montoya's mumbling. "We'll pretend we've just arrived, and offer her a ride to the beach."

"I don't want her in my boat. Why would we do that?"

"Because I have to rescue my cat. Weren't you listening? How else can we do it? And hitting her is *not* an option, Quill."

He frowned. "You sure? Okay. You're sure. You don't have to give me that look. It's creepy. It reminds me of Tricky when she's—"

"Yes, and all that. We're running out of time. And we still have more ships to look at."

"How 'bout this. We come in, tell her we'll return for her, and then we don't."

"You think that's a better idea?"

"Aye, 'cause otherwise we'll have to take her to the beach. And then what excuse will we use to leave the beach to search the other ships?"

He had a point.

"Fine. But I'll do the talking. You go stand guard on the deck or something."

Quill agreeably left me, and I cautiously approached the door from which Mrs. Montoya's voice sounded.

"And then you know what I'll do, little pussy?"

"I'd rather not think about it," Pooky whimpered.

"I'll set Wee Rodney down and tell him what's what."

I rapped my knuckles against the door. "Mrs. Montoya?"

The woman's prattling ceased.

"It's me."

"Who?"

"Miss Storm from *The Pink Pearl*. I noticed you moving around the ship on my way to the beach, and was wondering if you needed a ride."

She shuffled closer to the door. "Why do you care?"

An excellent question. "Us women have to stick together."

"Bah. I don't stick together with no one except me Rodney. You probably wanna hold me ransom, to blackmail the new king."

"That's quite imaginative of you."

"You mean sneaky and devious of you!" The door opened, and I stared into the muzzle of a pistol.

Chapter Twenty-Eight

"WELL?" Mrs. Montoya tightened her grip on her pistol, narrowing her flinty eyes. "Whatcha doin' here? Skulkin' 'round—"

"Madam, I most certainly do not skulk." I lifted my chin, determinedly ignoring the weapon pointed at my heart. "I was sleuthing. That's very different."

"Finally!" Pooky squealed. "I've been stuck here forever! Save me. Now."

"It's been a matter of minutes, Pooky," I said. "And I'm sure Mrs. Montoya was treating you with the utmost regard for your safety and..." I bit off my sentence before I said *dignity*. There was nothing dignified about Pooky's situation.

He was sitting in a baby's pram, a frilly bib around his neck, a tiny hat with a pom-pom on top tied between his ears, and a small, knitted cape wrapped around his shoulders.

He wiggled his whiskers. "You were saying?"

Mrs. Montoya snapped her jaw closed. "Sounds like ye talk to yer cat."

"Yes, I'm sure it does."

She looked me up and down. "You that stowaway?"

"To cut a long story short, yes."

Mrs. Montoya smirked. A thin mustache lined her top lip, and I couldn't stop staring at it.

"Somethin' the matter, love?"

I blinked, met her gaze and tried to smile. It felt like a grimace. "Nothing at all. I'm here to retrieve my cat."

"Yer cat, then?"

Pooky hissed. "I belong to no one. I'm a free, independent—"

"My mistake. I'll leave now," I said and started to back away.

"Yes, I'm hers. I'm hers!" Pooky leaped out of the pram and sprinted toward me, cape flapping behind him.

"Not so fast." Mrs. Montoya waved the gun at me and put out her leg to block Pooky's path. "How do I know he's really yers? Maybe you got catnip in yer pocket. Cats can't resist it. Fer all I know, he's an innocent stray, and you, a thief."

Pooky peered up at me, eyes bigger than I'd ever seen them. His whiskers quivered. "Don't leave me. I can't promise I'll behave, but I'll try not to spit hairballs into your tea."

"He has a stomach condition, you know," I confided. "The slightest wave, and he—" I mimed projectile vomiting.

"I have no such condition," Pooky squealed.

Mrs. Montoya glanced at Pooky, her expression souring, her lips puckering in distaste. "A sensitive one, eh?"

"The worst. I have to force-feed him medicine three times a day, five times if there's a storm."

"You don't say? So why were you and yer cat skulkin' 'round me ship?"

"You mean Captain Rodney's," I corrected, momentarily forgetting she held a gun pointed at me.

"What's his is mine."

"I was looking for my cat."

"A likely story. I think you'll be sittin' tight with me 'til the cap'n arrives. Rodney'll know what ta do with the likes of you."

Movement attracted my attention. An unusually large porthole above the bed was open to the sea breeze. Quill's head appeared. He held his bludgeon in one hand and waved it, mouthing something.

"Truth is, I'm trying to prove who really killed Sweetie," I confided and imperceptibly shook my head at Quill.

Quill frowned and wiggled partway through the porthole. He held out the arm holding the bludgeon and mimed hitting Mrs. Montoya.

"It's a terrible idea," I added.

"What is?" Mrs. Montoya took a step closer, squinting. "You're a strange one, you are."

"Quite so. Do you have any suspicions on who the real murderer is?"

Mrs. Montoya harrumphed and put away her pistol. "It sure ain't that miserable Winks fella. He's a softy, that one. Won't so much as set a rat trap. Sensitive soul. Don't know what he's doin' on this ship. Ain't no pirate like me Wee Rodney, that's fer sure."

"I'm sure not. Any other ideas? Anyone who might be interested in studying flowers?"

"Studying what? The idea! Though there's a flower collection on *The Dolphin's Kiss*."

"The king's ship?"

"The same."

"How extraordinary."

"Extra somethin', that's for sure. You want some tea?"

Quill fell through the porthole, collapsing on the bed.

I reached forward and held onto Mrs. Montoya's hand before she could turn around. "Bless you. For raising such a fine young man as your son. He deserves to be the pirate king."

Quill rolled off the mattress, shook himself and stood. He lifted his bludgeon.

"He does, don't he?" Mrs. Montoya nodded. "And I was a good mom, even if he don't appreciate all I've done."

I squeezed her hand and shook my head. "They never do, do they? Well, there's no need to knock ourselves over the head, now is there?"

Quill looked at his bludgeon, his shoulders slumping.

"So wise fer someone so young. Let's go to the galley. Make us a pot of tea."

"Marvelous." I stepped aside, waiting until she marched into the hallway. I waved at Quill. "Don't. Do. Anything."

"What?" he whispered back. "She was goin' to shoot you. Least I could do was knock her o'er the head."

"You comin', Miss Storm?"

"Right behind you," I called out and stepped into the hallway, still wagging my finger at Quill. I padded after Mrs. Montoya.

"What about me?" Pooky mewed, following me like a shadow. "I'm dressed like a human child. And not one of the nice human children. One of those small, squalling, smelly ones, the ones that can't walk."

"A baby?"

"Is that what you call them? Appalling. Kittens start walking within weeks of birth. But humans? Months. A year, even!"

"Set yerself here, love," Mrs. Montoya said, gesturing

to the mess hall. "I'll be a jiffy. We'll have a spot of tea, a good chat, and you happen to be lookin' fer a husband? Me Rodney's in need of a good woman, 'part from me, o' course."

Pooky almost tossed out a hairball right there and then. I smacked a hand over my mouth before my first response could blurt out. "How creative of you."

"That I am, love. Have a think 'bout it." She disappeared into the galley.

I scooped up Pooky and stepped back out into the hallway. Quill was just exiting Mrs. Montoya's cabin.

"Hurry up," I whispered and gestured to the exit.

"Milk or sugar?"

"None, thanks," I said.

"That's good. We're outa both. Have ta find us a merchant ship soon to restock."

"Good plan," I said.

Quill dashed past the galley, then walked backward, gesturing for me to follow him.

"Tea," I mouth and gestured to the galley.

Quill stopped, frowning. He pulled out his bludgeon. "Should I?"

"No!"

He shrugged and disappeared outside. I gave him a full thirty seconds before I forced a cheerful smile and appeared in the galley's doorway. "On second thought, Mrs. Montoya, can we do this another time? I need to attend to an urgent matter. My cat! He hasn't had his medicine yet."

Pooky let forth a pitiful yowl, his head sagging dramatically against my arm.

"The poor love. Go on, then, Miss Storm. But you promised. We'll catch up soon, eh?"

"We'll catch something," I said and ran after Quill.

Chapter Twenty-Nine

"I CAN'T BELIEVE the king killed Sweetie," I muttered as Quill rowed the boat over to *The Dolphin's Kiss*.

"Oi, Miss Storm. We don't know it was Brownbeard. Could be anyone had a grudge against Sweetie. He wasn't much liked."

"Be that as it may, the fingers all point to the king. For a start, owning a flower collection requires some resources. And remember how anxious he was to solve this case before the elections? Everything that's happened has eliminated his opponents in some way. Captain Rodney looks bad because he didn't protect his previous quartermaster, and his new quartermaster was arrested for murder."

"What about Pepe? His name's also on the list."

"True. But Scotty told me the incumbent always has an advantage, especially if he's also a captain. Who will pirates vote for, a captain who's already the king? Or his quartermaster?"

Quill shrugged. "Depends. Pepe's well liked. He's smart. An excellent swordsman. Worked his way up the ranks, so he knows how a ship works from bottom to top."

"I suppose. But he didn't seem particularly fussed one way or the other about the rankings."

"You may be right. It's not too strange for pirate kings to eliminate the opposition."

"So much for a peace pact."

He grinned. "It's been pretty peaceful, all things considered. Only one person died this time."

"This is a regular occurrence?"

"More or less. We're competin' with each other most o' the year. It's nothin' short of a miracle we spend three days without jumpin' at each other's throats. Though nothin' beats the fifty-first for disaster."

"That's hardly comforting."

"Hope Mrs. Montoya's right." He nodded at the horizon. "The election'll be soon. Sun's close to setting."

"We'll find out soon enough."

The rowboat gently bumped against *The Dolphin's Kiss*. It was the biggest ship in the harbor. It had three levels instead of two. I almost asked Quill if the pirates looked at the size of the ship when voting. I held my tongue. I didn't really want to hear Quill explain the intricacies of voting, or what they looked for.

The rope ladder was sturdier than what I was used to. I managed to climb to the deck without banging my knees against the hull.

"Sure's quiet," Quill said as he joined me. "I was expectin' a guard or two." He thumped his bludgeon against the palm of one hand to emphasize what he planned to do if we found any guards.

"No thumping. If we see anyone, we'll tell them we're lost."

"Lost? You think anyone'll believe that?"

"If I bat my eyelashes and start to cry?"

Quill gave me a onceover. "Aye. That they'd believe. Very connivin' o' you. You're becomin' quite the pirate."

"I'm sure you mean that as a compliment, but let's focus on the mission, shall we? We'll have to split up."

"Think that's a good idea?" Quill asked. "You might really get lost."

"It's a terrible idea," Pooky said. "This whole adventure's a bad dream from which I hope to wake. But who listens to the cat? Especially one still dressed like a human baby. This is humiliating."

"It'll be fine. We don't have time."

Quill didn't look convinced, and Pooky made his opinion abundantly clear. Quill took the top level where the dormitories and most of the crew slept. I headed for the lowest level, and we agreed to meet somewhere in the middle.

"Pooky, let me know if you hear or smell anything," I said.

He spat. "I smell plenty, and none of it pleasant."

"I mean *dangerous* sounds and smells, like someone sneaking up behind me."

"Oh. That might be difficult. It's stinky enough in here I can barely smell myself, and I smell marvelous."

I headed toward the end of the bottom level, passing by a pantry that was bigger than *The Pink Pearl*'s galley. I then saw a galley that must be the envy of all pirate ships. Down another corridor were various officer quarters, each quite grand in comparison to anything I'd seen. But no sign of a flower collection.

"Can you smell any flowers?" I asked.

Pooky's claws pricked against my skin. "Do I look like a dog?"

"No, but your nose is more sensitive than mine."

"You mean superior, and that goes without saying. Did

it ever occur to you that Mrs. Montoya might not be fully stable, even by human standards?"

"Why would she lie?"

"I can think of at least half a dozen reasons."

I opened another door. "Please illuminate me."

"To protect her son, for a start. If the king is implicated, Rodney will most likely be voted in."

"A fair point. What about the other five?"

Pooky wriggled out of my arms and flopped onto a writing desk. "That was it. All my reasons."

"I suppose counting isn't your strongest suit."

"Why do I need to count? I'm a cat."

I crossed the hall. The next cabin clearly belonged to Brownbeard. It was large, even by wealthy Londoner standards. A painting filled up most of one wall. Brownbeard rode a galloping horse on a beach, sword held up victoriously.

"They forgot to include his double chin," Pooky said. "Give me some ink. I'll fix this painting."

I scooped Pooky up and studied the cabin for any sign of flowers. "No vandalism allowed."

"Not even a little?"

"None at all."

"That's no fun. You have to agree with me. The painter utterly failed to capture the king's pouty expression, his saggy double chin and squashed eyes. He almost looks handsome in this painting. By human standards, of course."

"That's the point of a portrait. To make you look your best for posterity."

"You're right. His posterior's also not painted correctly. His is so much bigger and plumper and—"

"Nothing here." I stepped into the hallway. There was

one door left at the very end. I eased it open, holding my breath.

No botany collection or even a flower in a vase greeted my eager gaze. Only another officer's cabin. I sagged on the bed, wondering what to do next. Perhaps Quill had more luck. Or maybe it was on the second level.

"This smells disgustinger," Pooky said and swatted at something under the bed.

"There's no such word as disgustinger."

"There is now. I created it. Because I can do that. It smelled disgusting before. It's even more disgusting now. Hence, disgustinger."

"What smells disgusting?"

"Do I look like a botany expert?"

I slid off the bed and onto my knees. The bed had a couple of long, narrow drawers underneath it. It was a system I'd seen in all the other officers' cabins. Apart from the king's quarters, few people had the luxury of space. Every bit of it was utilized as efficiently and as effectively as possible.

I pulled on the bottom drawer and slid it out. Sunlight from the porthole glinted off a sheet of glass. And under the glass was a vast collection of pressed flowers.

"Hello, there," I whispered.

"Do you actually expect those flowers to talk back to you?" Pooky sighed. "You know they're dead. And even if they weren't, they won't greet you in return. Flowers are snobbish that away. Always keeping to themselves. Not at all interested in returning one's greetings. Rude little things, I say. That's why I have no regrets about shredding their flimsy little petals."

I scanned the collection. No sign of *Decaying Corpses*. But it definitely indicated a certain interest and expertise in the study of flowers. I slid the drawer back and pulled out the next one. Again, more flowers. They were from all over the known world, meticulously documented with neatly written labels underneath each pressed flower. Their Latin name, their common name and the location where they were found.

"We have to find out whose cabin this is." I stood up, kicking the door shut.

"Definitely a man," Pooky said.

"Obviously, since everyone here is male apart from me, Mrs. Montoya and Tricky."

"There's no need to be uptight about it. I was simply providing you information about the dweller of this cabin. He also likes perfume. Or maybe that's from the flowers in his desk."

I went to the writing desk. "I don't know if I should be infuriated with you, or grateful you're here."

"Grateful, of course. Is there any doubt about it?"

I rummaged through the drawers and cubbyholes. In the third drawer was a couple of wilting specimens of *Decaying Corpses*. A thick diary underneath the petals caught my attention. Inside was the amateur botanist's name on the first page, followed by detailed notes of his discoveries.

"There's no doubt now," I said. "We have to find Quill. We need a witness."

"I don't think that'll be necessary, Miss Storm."

I gasped and spun around, bumping my hip painfully against the desk. But the pain was nothing compared to my shock as Pepe Le Pirate leveled his pistol at my chest.

Chapter Thirty

I GAWKED AT THE PISTOL. "Well, this is a conundrum."

Pepe leaned casually against the doorjamb, unperturbed by my discovery. "I figured you were up to no good when I didn't see you at the beach."

"And I've just figured out you're the murderer."

Pepe bowed slightly, his mouth twisting into a cruel smirk. "It was my pleasure to rid the pirate world of such a terrible member."

"I suppose it doesn't hurt that this whole sorry affair has pushed you up in the rankings."

He gave me a mock innocent look. "Has it now? We didn't notice. But yes, it removes that bumbling Brownbeard and the even more incompetent Rodney from the ballot. Unfortunately, we now have a dilemma."

"Why's he talking in the royal *we*?" Pooky asked. "You'd think he's a descendent of a god or a king the way he speaks. Make sure to tell him he's a mere commoner, and a human to boot."

"We'll have to arrange an unfortunate event," Pepe continued, ignoring Pooky's meows and irritated hisses.

"The only unfortunate event to arrange is you walking the plank," I said.

"I think not. After all, *you* were the one who snuck onto the ship of the pirate king. Oh, that won't look good, either. Brownbeard doesn't stand a chance now."

"I didn't sneak. He requested me to investigate the murder—"

"Which was solved this morning for the second time, thanks to you. You eliminated the other candidate in the process. So what business do you now have on this ship except mischief and mayhem?"

"That's not really my style."

Pooky snorted. "It really isn't. Look at the way she's dressed. No style at all. How much longer is he going to talk? I don't want to miss the feast."

I summoned the *La Look* I'd developed with Tricky, but it felt wilted. Its lack of force had something to do with a loaded pistol in the hands of a murderer standing a few feet from me. "Everyone'll know you're a liar. I'll tell them what I found here."

"It doesn't matter. You're the stowaway. The story I'll share is remarkably simple. You snuck onto the ship and into my cabin. You were rummaging through my items, with the intent of thievery or some other malpractice."

"You should be very familiar with such activities yourself."

"Yes. The difference is I don't get caught."

"Except now."

"A minor inconvenience. I wasn't finished with the story. Now, here's what's going to happen."

"Is this human planning on talking you to death?" Pooky asked.

Movement behind Pepe distracted me. I gazed over his

shoulder as Quill tiptoed into view. For a big man, he could certainly move in a stealthy fashion.

Pooky clawed at the locked porthole. "Can you unlock this for me?"

"I'm going to set a small fire outside this door," Pepe intoned.

"You're going to burn your own ship?" I raised my voice in case Quill stepped on any squeaky boards.

"Oh, no. I rather like this ship, especially once I'm king. It's only a small fire. Nothing too dramatic. Just enough to fill this cabin with smoke, leave a few burns, and char the wood. You didn't only come here to steal from us but also to commit sabotage."

"Why would I do that?"

Pepe shrugged. "One never knows with malcontents such as yourself. After all, you stowed away on a pirate ship. These aren't the actions of a sane woman."

"He makes a decent point there," Pooky said.

"I didn't ask you," I muttered.

"Actually, you did." Pepe frowned. "Maybe you really *are* mad. In which case, this whole scene's much more believable. I have again saved the pirating world from another disastrous member."

"I'm *not* a pirate."

"No, you're a witch," Pooky reminded me. "Speaking of which, can you do anything about this? Cast a spell. Turn him into a bowl of cream."

My hand slid toward my pocket where the vial of fresh-water rested.

"No, no, no." Pepe waved his pistol. "Keep your hands where I can see them, Miss Storm."

Quill now stood almost immediately behind Pepe. He held up his bludgeon and pointed at it, mouthing something.

"I really don't understand you," I said.

Quill pointed vigorously at his bludgeon, then mimed hitting the wall.

"There's not much to understand, my dear." Pepe shook his head. "In fact, it's rather straightforward. I'm not sure why you're having such difficulties."

"I suppose you're difficult to understand. What're you doing?"

Quill rolled his eyes and held up both arms, waving the bludgeon toward Pepe.

"Stop dawdling and get on with it, then," I snapped.

"As you will," Pepe said.

"Finally," Quill muttered and swung the bludgeon at Pepe's head.

Pepe jerked to one side, and the bludgeon glanced off of his shoulder. He winced, almost dropping his pistol as he stumbled away from Quill.

"Been waitin' to do that for a long time." Quill lunged at Pepe, following him into the cabin.

Pepe easily dodged Quill's clumsy efforts and stepped back into the doorway, gun held in a trembling hand. "You brought this buffoon with you? It doesn't matter. This'll make an even better story. The two of you, secretly lovers—"

"Absolutely not," I huffed.

"I can live with that," Quill said. "Does it have to be secret?"

"You won't live for long, so enjoy your affair while it lasts." Pepe slammed the door shut, and a key turned in the lock.

"You heard the man. Let's enjoy." Quill sat on the bed and patted the mattress next to him. "Isn't this cozy?"

"No, and it's going to get a lot less cozy and a lot more

heated in a moment." I immediately regretted my choice of words.

Quill's grin widened. "Aye! That's what I like to hear, Miss Storm."

"I think he's been hit one too many times on the head with that stick thing." Pooky scratched at the porthole. "Why won't this open? I want to leave."

I eyed the porthole. It was too small for anyone but a cat to squeeze through. But why should Pooky suffer? I worked on the porthole's latch, but it was jammed shut.

"I'm too young and beautiful to die!" the cat wailed, clawing at the glass.

My nose twitched. "Do you smell something funny?"

"I smell many things, none of which are funny," Pooky said.

"It must be the flowers." I closed the drawer with the *Decaying Corpses*.

Quill stood. "No, it smells like..." He inhaled deeply. "Smoke."

A flicker of motion caught my attention. Tendrils of smoke curled underneath the door. "He's going to suffocate us to death. We have to get out of here."

Quill wiggled the handle and pressed his shoulder against it. "We're not going out this way. It's heavy wood, and a strong lock."

"Let me try." I removed my lock pick set, grateful I never left home without it.

"Did I ever tell you you're magnificent? A natural-born pirate, you are."

"Save it for when we escape and tell everyone who the real murderer is."

"You need to consider a career as a pirate, Miss Storm. Best job in the Old World. Pillage, plunder and the pirate way, plus relaxed rules and generous benefits."

"Hmm. Sounds enticing."

"You'll join, then?"

"No." I worked on the lock. It took longer than usual. Quill was right. It was a high-quality door, and a high-quality lock.

Meanwhile, more smoke came inside, faster, thicker, and straight up my nose. I coughed, my eyes watering.

"Enjoy your last few minutes," Pepe shouted. "I'll be back soon with other pirates to save the ship from being burned by you two vandalizers."

"The word's vandal, not vandalizer," Quill yelled and thumped a fist against the wall.

The lock *snicked* open.

"I wouldn't open that door, if I were you," Pooky said from his perch on the porthole's sill.

"Hah! And why not?" I asked as I triumphantly pulled the door open.

A thick cloud of blinding smoke billowed into the cabin, choking me with its acrid smell. Coughing, I slammed the door shut and leaned against it.

"That's why," Pooky said.

"You see a fire out there?" Quill asked and pressed his hand against the wood.

"I didn't see anything but smoke."

"I can't smell a thing," Pooky said. "That flower is disgusting."

"We have to risk it," Quill said. "I'll wrap us in a blanket and carry you. It'll be romantic. If we die, we'll be in each other's arms at the end. A fitting pirate death."

"That's not romantic, Quill. That's horrific."

He shrugged. "Or we stay here and wait for the smoke to smother us."

"I have another idea." I reached for my water vial.

Pooky hissed. "I'm not a witch. But I believe your laws

require you to hide your true identity from humans. Especially uninitiated humans. And this thick-headed Romeo definitely counts as uninitiated, uninformed, uneducated—"

"I get the point."

Quill grinned. "So I pick you up and run through the flames?"

I held up the water vial. "Can you keep a secret?"

Quill's smile softened, and he patted my shoulder. "I already know. You've been secretly in love with me from the first day. I haven't told a soul, Miss Storm. Not a one. Even when the other blokes were talkin' 'bout you. I kept it to myself."

I brushed his hand off my shoulder. "You're cute, but no. I mean another secret."

"No! Don't tell me. You're in love with Scotty? He said as much."

"No, and when?" I held up a hand. "Don't. It doesn't matter. My cat's an anxious creature."

Pooky jerked his head up, his eyes narrowed. "I don't like where this is going."

"He was orphaned as a young kitten."

"You're using *me* as the distraction? That's low, even for you."

I leaned closer to Quill. "Do you think you can hold him, show him the open ocean outside that porthole, and reassure him it's going to be okay?"

Quill's frown burrowed into his forehead, leaving deep furrows in its wake. "You're worried about the *cat?*"

"You bet she's worried about the cat," Pooky grumbled. "I'm an important entity, and—"

"If you don't calm him down, he'll cause a big stink. And then I can't check outside to see if there's a fire or not."

Quill's skepticism deepened.

I looked up at the ceiling, praying for intervention from the gods of stranded witches. "The truth is, I need a moment to myself. To vent my frail, feminine emotions." I almost choked on the words. If Grand Dame Puddlewick could hear me now, she'd curse me ten times over and turn me into a toad.

Quill sighed. "Of course. Have your moment. Then we shall do our best to run through the flames. May they burn as brightly as our love."

"Exactly. Or not."

He turned his back on me, and I on him. I only had enough water in the vial for one spell. Which one to use? A cold wind to clear the smoke? A heavy ocean wave to douse the flames?

"I was thinkin'," Quill said.

"Please don't," Pooky muttered. "It's painful to watch."

"Yes, Quill?"

"Maybe we can toss these blankets on the fire and smother it. Might not work, but—"

I capped the vial. "You're almost brilliant at times."

"Thank you. I try not to be, but occasionally, it just happens."

I helped Quill rip off the bedding. Heavy quilts, a blanket, a couple of sheets and the mattress. "This might work."

"Please hurry," Pooky said. "My eyes are starting to tear up. Bloodshot eyes are *not* a good look for a cat."

Quill ripped one of the sheets and offered me a piece. "Put this around your nose and mouth."

"Stop," I said. "You're starting to really impress me now."

"It comes naturally. That mask looks good on you.

You'd make a great-lookin' pirate. Or a vagabond, at least."

"I'll keep it in mind when considering my career choices in the New World. Shall we?"

We opened the door, hopefully better prepared. The smoke was thicker and managed to leak around our bandannas. But the fire wasn't particularly big, just as Pepe had promised. We tossed the mattress and the blankets into the hallway, and immediately the smoke settled.

Quill patted me heavily on the back. "Good job."

"Good idea."

"Good gracious, it's about time." Pooky snaked between our legs, his tail whipping back and forth. "I'm officially fed up with life as a pirate. Do you hear me? Exasperated, even. I'm going back home. If someone would be kind enough to sail in that direction, I might be grateful enough to allow him or her to stroke my back."

Quill turned around and frowned. "It's almost sunset."

I nodded and plucked a hair off of a pillow. "Then it's time to stop an election and catch a murderer."

Chapter Thirty-One

PERHAPS IT WAS the aftereffects of the smoke, but it was annoying nonetheless. Quill continued to trip over himself in order to demonstrate the pirate way of romance. It was a form of chivalry I'd never seen before, and I was fed up with it by the time we reached the rope ladder.

He attempted to toss me over his shoulder so I wouldn't blister my hands. I threw a cat at his head. The cat wasn't amused. Quill simply laughed it off.

Instead of rowing hard for shore, he set a leisurely pace until I reminded him that sunset was minutes away.

"And if you tell me that I'm your sunset or moonrise or any other such romantic nonsense, I'll toss the cat at you again."

"You'd better not," Pooky snarled. "I'm still recovering from the first time."

We arrived with no time to spare. The bonfire was lit, the pirates were engaged in chaotic revelry, a couple of fireflies floated overhead, and the king was attempting to get everyone's attention.

"Made it," Quill said. "Nothin' to worry about."

"Except they're about to vote. Let's go." I didn't wait for Quill to prove his devotion or whatever he was doing. I pushed through the excited crowd. Misty, my sister, always said I had sharp elbows. I put those to good use, and for good measure held out in front of me a thoroughly enraged cat.

"I'm definitely going to eat that egg," Pooky vowed.

"Do you want to go home, or walk the plank?"

Pooky hissed loudly and slashed his claws at any pirate too slow to get out of my way.

"Miss Storm!"

I froze, wondering if Pepe had made his announcement yet. "Please lower your voice, Scotty."

"Aye. Still time to place your bets," he yelled as he sidled up to me. "A few pirates've already dropped out o' the runnin'. One o' them 'cause he's in the pit, awaitin' his fate. The others don't stand a real hope, and—"

"Who are the frontrunners?" I asked.

"Pepe and the pirate king are neck to neck. Rodney's laggin' behind, but there's them that still favor him. Want to place a wee wager?"

"I suspect I know who's going to win," I said and hurried toward the throne. "Your Majesty!"

"My fellow pirates, save the king! There are traitors among us!" Pepe came running up from the beach. We had arrived before him only because he'd stopped for a costume change. He looked dreadful, his shirt tattered and stained, a bruise blossoming on his chin, and a bandage around his hand.

"Course there be traitors," Stinker shouted back. "We're pirates!"

"Hurrah!"

"No. I mean her, and her lover." Pepe staggered in front of the fire, standing between me and the king. His quivering finger pointed at me, then at Quill. If he looked surprised to see us alive, he didn't show it.

"What nonsense is this?" Tricky demanded, marching to my side.

"'Tis true," Quill said. "We're lovers."

"No, we're not. It's a story he's making up. Remember, Quill?"

Quill scowled, Pepe sneered, and the pirates all stepped back, creating an open circle with me, Quill, Pepe and Tricky in the center. We'd arrived just in time to give them a before-dinner show.

"Well, speak up, man," Brownbeard commanded.

"It's true, your Barbaric Exaltedness," Pepe said, out of breath as if he'd swum all the way from the ship. "I found them on *The Dolphin's Kiss*, rummaging through our cabins, and preparing to set a fire! I arrived in time to save the ship, but these vandals beat me up for my efforts."

"I doubt it took two of them to do that," Tricky drawled.

"Hurrah!"

Pepe's accusatory finger shifted toward Tricky. "You. You always were troublesome. Now you're defending the stowaway and her vandal lover?"

"At least he got the word right," Quill said.

"Don't even think of tossing me at him," Pooky hissed. "It won't be pretty."

"Well, well," the king said. "This is quite a conundrum."

"Not really, your Royal Highness." I tried stepping around Pepe, but he kept blocking my path. "I found the poison that killed Sweetie."

"'Twas a knife that killed him," Rodney said.

"No. A poison from a very special flower, one that only

a highly skilled, extremely knowledgeable and intelligent botanist can recognize."

Pepe started to preen at the compliment, then realized what he was doing and shook his head. "You're the stowaway. You're behind it all. Trying to make my king look bad."

"She doesn't have to try hard," Pooky meowed.

"She's always skulking around—"

"I don't skulk."

"And always with that black cat." Pepe gasped. "I wouldn't be surprised if she be a witch!"

A mixture of gasps and hurrahs peppered the crowd.

"Said so 'fore, didn't I?" Stubbs added.

"Whatever you may call me, I have proof you were behind the murder."

"Lies! You've gravely insulted me and besmirched my name."

The pirates took another step away from me as Pepe pulled out a sword.

"I'll handle this, Miss Storm," Quill said and started to remove his sword.

"What are you doing?" I demanded. "We'll settle this the civilized way."

"Aye, we shall. This is the pirate way." With that, Quill flourished his sword, and Pepe did the same.

Flustered, I faced the king. "Does no one want to see the proof?"

"Very well. If you must." The king waved me forward. "Hold those swords for a moment, mateys. Seems we have to deal with a landlubber's version of court proceedings."

The pirates laughed, and Scotty pulled out a notebook. "Place your bets while you can. Will there be a duel? Who'll win? Will Miss Storm and her secret lover prevail?

Is she a witch? Will the king cut off her head? So many options. So little time."

I turned in the middle of the circle and reached into my bag. "Behold. Pepe Le Pirate's diary." I pulled it out and held it above my head.

"Pepe can write?" Scribblers asked.

"He has a diary?" The king shook his head. "What sort of pirates have we become? Writing and keeping a diary. A diary! What next, a novel? Appalling. I'm disappointed, Pepe."

Pepe bowed. "It's not mine, sir."

I opened the first page, cleared my throat and read, "This diary belongs to Pepe Le Pirate, also known in some circles as Pepe Le Fleur d'Odor."

"No wonder he changed his name," Scotty shouted, to jeers and laughs.

Pepe grew red in the face. "How dare you. How dare——"

"May I?" Scribbles stepped toward me, his hand out.

I handed over the book. Silence descended across the beach. It felt as if everyone was holding their breath or at least their tongues.

Scribbles flipped through the pages, scanning the contents. "She speaks the truth. It's his diary. He's a botanist. And there's a recipe here entitled *How to make a quick-acting poison using a poisonous flower found on the island named Treasure.*"

More gasps, a few hurrahs, and a very loud hiss from the cat sitting on my feet.

"Lies, all lies," Pepe said, backing away.

"Why did you do such a thing?" the king asked.

"To make you look bad, your Royal Beardness," I said. "He framed Winks to make Rodney look bad, thus eliminating two candidates with the most potential for winning the throne. He planted the knife to confuse the case even more."

"The lass has it right," Scotty said. "Brownbeard was first in the rankings 'til the murder, then Rodney went up but fell back when his new quartermaster was discovered with Sweetie's sugar. Only Pepe has been steadily gaining in the polls."

"Release Winks at once," Rodney said with a triumphant smile. "I knew he was innocent."

I didn't argue. Winks would be so grateful to be released that he wouldn't hold it against his own captain for turning his back on him.

"Blasted barnacles," Stubbs said. "I was lookin' forward to a good plankin'."

"But we'll still have one," Scotty said. "This time with the real murderer."

"Hurrah!"

I looked around. "Speaking of which."

Pepe Le Pirate was gone.

Chapter Thirty-Two

"WHERE IS PEPE LE PIRATE?" the king bellowed.

"Seems like he's run off," Scotty said. "Guess he ain't a candidate anymore."

"Blast 'im with a cannon," Stubbs grumbled. "A week's worth o' wages, gone."

"Never you mind," Scribbles said. "The election shall go forth, as is the tradition. The sixty-second pirate parlay shall not be delayed. Thus it has been decreed."

"Hurrah!"

"What if he tries to poison someone again?" I pointed at the jungle. "There are plenty more *Decaying Corpses* in there."

Scotty turned to Tricky. "How many people has he killed?"

Tricky clamped her teeth around her pipe. "Only the one, Scotty."

"Disappointin'. But I s'pose you have to start somewhere."

"Aren't we going after him?" I looked around, waiting

for the pirates to hurrah and flash their swords over their heads.

Scribbles pulled out a pocket watch. "According to tradition, the vote must happen within a few minutes after sunset. There's no time to run amok through the jungle. Thus it has been decreed."

"But—"

"Don't you worry, lass," Scotty said and wrapped an arm around my shoulders, ignoring Quill's glare. "It's not like he can go anywhere. We're on an island! Ain't that right, mateys?"

"Hurrah!"

"Then let the voting commence," the pirate king intoned.

"Hurrah!"

"This is ludicrous," I said.

Pooky signed. "You're telling me. We missed morning *and* afternoon tea. Whatever happened to the civilized habit of giving one's cat a saucer of cream?"

"I'm going after Pepe."

"Have fun." Pooky curled up on Quill's boots.

"Aren't you coming with me?"

"Evidently not. Hey, unhand me!"

I jogged through the excited crowd of pirates, ignoring Scotty's plea to place a bet. The cat bounced on my shoulders, hissing threats in my ear.

Quill ran after me. "Miss Storm, it's not safe in the jungle."

"It's not safe anywhere, so I hardly think it matters where I am."

"Listen to the brainless brute," Pooky said. "He has a point. It's a jungle. Let the murderous pirate hide in there by himself."

Quill snatched my hand and pulled me around. I

bumped against his chest, then staggered backward, peering up at him in amazement.

"Miss Storm, I may not've made my feelings clear to you—"

"I'm quite sure you have. Far too clearly."

"But you're truly a miracle among women."

"It doesn't take much, given there aren't many women here."

"Stay with me." Quill thumped a fist over his heart. "I'll swashbuckle my way across the three oceans—"

"There're four, actually."

"And duel for your honor at every opportunity."

"How… romantic."

"I feel a hairball coming up," Pooky grunted, coughing spasmodically.

"I need to go now," I said.

"Why're you so determined to capture Pepe?"

I paused, mulling over the question. It was more than tempting to return to the cheerful fire and witness a historical event, pirates voting in their new king.

But something compelled me. Pride? Maybe a sense that my job wasn't done. Plus, I wanted to satisfy the king's demand and prove to Tricky I was useful. To avoid my fate as the hundredth and one wife or concubine of Chief Ali Babak, I needed to finish this job.

"Sorry, Quill." I yanked my hand out of his grasp and ran into the jungle, a howling cat over my shoulder.

"I'm comin' with you," Quill shouted.

"So am I, lass," Scotty cheerfully called out.

"I've already placed my claim, sailing master."

"And I'm placing mine, you quarter of a master!"

"Maybe we should keep running," Pooky said.

"A brilliant idea."

I ducked behind a tree and pulled out my vial. "Time to try the seeker spell."

"Try? Try! You mean you don't know how to do that?"

"I never quite mastered it."

"And what happens if you fail?"

"A small explosion."

Pooky whimpered.

"Don't worry. I'll toss you behind me before it happens." I held out the hair I'd plucked from Pepe's pillow and dropped it into the vial of water. I then began chanting the seeker spell. "*Finders, keepers, soldiers, seekers. Guide me by the witching light. To the soul I seek to right.*"

The water bubbled, frothing at the opening.

"Miss Storm?" Scotty cried out.

"Miss Storm, come back," Quill said.

"She's runnin' away from you, you know."

"You're wrong, sailor boy. We've been through a lot, her and me. We're perfectly suited."

"May the gods save me from enthusiastic suitors," I muttered.

A curl of shiny blue steam twirled out of the vial, then twitched back and forth, sniffing at the air. It lunged forward, tugging me in a direction that I hoped led me to Pepe Le Pirate.

"It worked!"

"I don't know how you managed for so long," Pooky groaned as I set out at a sprint. "I have nine lives, and I can barely keep up with you."

The glimmering blue curl kept tugging this way and that. It didn't lead me deeper into the jungle but parallel to the beach. I could hear the pirates shouting out yay or nay as each candidate was presented. It was a verbal vote, and I didn't envy Scribbles the job of keeping track or measuring who had the loudest vote.

"He must be heading for a rowboat," I said.

"You might want to slow down," Pooky said and sniffed delicately.

"No time."

"No, I really think—" Pooky punctuated the sentence with a shrill shriek that echoed my scream.

We slid down a muddy slope, smashing through bushes and long grass. At one point I was facing uphill, and I met Quill's astonished gaze from the top of the slope.

"Don't worry, Miss Storm. I'm coming for you."

"Not worried," I shouted right before my backside hit the water.

"Save me!" Pooky mewed pitifully. "Murky water. Yuck. It smells. My poor paws are brown." He scrambled up my back, digging his claws in.

"It's a swamp," I said. I checked the water vial. It wasn't broken, and neither was the spell. The blue curl tugged deeper into the swamp.

"Don't even think about it," Pooky said. "My nose has a really bad feeling about this."

"Your nose has a bad feeling about everything."

"True. But this is an extra-bad, extra-smelly feeling."

I waded deeper into the swamp. "We'll be fine. There's nothing here we need to fear."

"Except crocodiles and giant dogs."

"Do you see any of those?"

"No."

"Then we'll be fine."

"We're definitely going to die."

Chapter Thirty-Three

QUILL CAUGHT up to me when I was thigh deep in swampy water. He grinned and winked, holding up a lantern. "Scotty turned back. More interested in the election results than in courtship. Guess I won."

"What exactly did you win?" I asked.

"Your hand, o' course."

"I prefer to keep both of my hands, if you don't mind."

Quill frowned at the vial of water. "That's weird."

I stuffed the vial in my pocket. "What is?"

"That blue light."

"Swamp gas. It's a common phenomenon. How brave of you to join me here."

The distraction worked. Quill was all smiles and winks.

"I smell something," Pooky said.

I patted his head. "Do you hear anything, Quill?"

Pooky nudged my hand. "I said smell, not hear. Although now that you mention it, there's a lot of noise up ahead."

Quill tilted his head, his hand dropping to his sword. "Aye. You stay back, Miss Storm. I'll handle this."

"Again with the hands. I'll be fine. Follow me." I led the way through marshy grass, wincing every time my poor, delicate shoes squelched in the muck at the bottom. We exited the swamp just as Pepe ran toward us.

"That was easy," I said.

Eyes wide, Pepe screamed, "Save me!"

"A man after my own heart," Pooky said. "Remember I told you about a giant carnivore living in the jungle?"

A wild, savage-looking creature leaped out of the bushes, sharp canines glinting. It looked like the oversized offspring of a hyena and a bear. Its steeply sloping back and long, shaggy fur added to its frightful appearance.

"I now realize I was mistaken," Pooky continued. "There's more than one."

As if on cue, several other rabid-looking, mutated hyenas stalked out of the jungle, eyes shifting from Pepe to me.

"Miss Storm?" Quill touched my elbow, apparently afraid to reach for my hand. "Them's Nandi Bears. Those brain-eatin' Kerit I told you 'bout. Like the one that ate Stubbs' leg."

"It seems I owe you an apology," I said. "They're real, after all."

"Aye. Shall we leave now?"

"An excellent suggestion."

I turned and ran back to the swamp, Quill behind me, and Pepe a distant third.

"Don't leave me, you traitors," Pepe squealed.

I glanced back, wondering if I could create a spell using the swamp water. But there was no time.

Quill came to an abrupt halt in front of me. My nose smacked into his shoulder blade.

"A little warning next time," I lectured.

Pepe bounced against me, and all three of us tumbled and fell to our knees.

"And this was my one good dress," I said before looking up.

A large, scaled reptile eased off the shore and into the water.

"Is that a crocodile?" I asked.

Quill stood, reaching down for my hand. "Aye, Miss Storm. It is."

"Marvelous!" I stood up, cupping water in my hands.

Quill glanced at me and sighed. "This is what happens when young lassies go runnin' 'round in the hot sun. Stay behind me."

I rolled my eyes but said nothing. Crocodiles were water creatures, or rather they spent a good deal of time in the water. And I was a water witch.

I bent low over my cupped hands and whispered, "*Croc, that over cold sand lies. Day and night it blinks its eyes. Swimming past, give me air. Chase the Kerit yonder there.*"

The crocodile's tail swished violently, churning water as it raced past us. It opened its jaws and snapped at the closest Nandi Bear. The beast whimpered and splashed out of the water, racing back into the jungle, followed by its pack members.

"Weird," Quill said. "Was sure I had to fight it. Too bad."

I let the water fall out of my hands. "Yes, such a pity."

Chapter Thirty-Four

THE ELECTION WAS over by the time we returned with Pepe in tow.

"Brownbeard won the election," I said as we joined Scotty and Tricky.

"Aye, lassie. How'd you know?"

I glanced up at the pirate king's wide smile. "A lucky guess?"

The smile disappeared the moment he saw Pepe. "You! A traitor among traitors."

Pepe lifted his chin, but he still looked disheveled and frantic. His close call with the Nandi Bear pack and the crocodile had left him shaking and unusually quiet.

"Walk the plank," Quill intoned.

"Walk the plank!" the other pirates chanted. "Walk. The. Plank!"

Pepe's shoulders sagged. "It's as much as I deserve, your Majestic Terribleness."

"I can't watch," I said, covering my eyes.

"It's just a wee bit o' water," Scotty said. "It's not like

we're makin' him walk the plank in shark-infested seas. Now that's a rare sight to behold. And terrible indeed."

"Am I missing something about this whole plank deal?" Pooky asked.

"You and me both," I said under my breath.

The pirates continued chanting "Walk the plank!" as they crowded around Pepe and hoisted him on their shoulders.

"He looks upset, but not like a man about to die," Pooky continued his commentary.

I trailed behind the crowd, wondering if I should retreat to my tent and pack up. Curiosity compelled me down the fire-lit beach.

Several of the pirates piled into one of the larger rowboats and yanked Pepe inside. He sighed and gazed wistfully at the beach as the pirates rowed a couple of dozen meters away from shore.

The rest of the pirates lined up along the beach, chanting, "Walk the plank! Walk the—"

The pirate king strode in front of them and put up a fist. Silence reigned. "We have spoken. The will of the pirate brethren is clear. For his crimes against the throne, we—"

"Not to mention murder," I said, then winced as several pirates shushed me.

"As I was saying." The king cleared his throat and frowned at me. "For his crimes against the throne, and for the lesser crime of murder most exotic, we hereby condemn Pepe Le Pirate to walk the plank."

Scribbles called out, "Thus it has been decreed as per the laws set out by the Pirate Codex."

"Walk the plank!"

"Not much of a plank, is it?" Pooky asked.

VERED EHSANI

"Indeed not." Absentmindedly I stroked under his chin, and he purred loudly.

A small plank jutted out from the rowboat. Two of the pirates held it steady while two more pirates pushed Pepe onto it. At the accompaniment of more cheers and jeers, Pepe gulped and slowly tottered to the end, his arms tied behind him.

"Jump! Jump, jump, jump!" the crowd shouted.

Pepe closed his eyes, tipped his head back, and stepped off the plank into neck-high water. The pirates cheered, laughing and calling Pepe names.

I turned to Quill and Scotty. "That's it?"

Scotty frowned. "Aye. What were you expectin', lass? That we'd string him up and toss him to the sharks? That'd require a grievous crime indeed."

"Because murder isn't?"

Tricky puffed on her pipe heavily, her face shrouded in sweet-scented smoke. "When it comes to Sweetie, it was only a matter of time."

Pepe stumbled out of the water, dripping and taking the jokes good-naturedly. I wondered if he would remain as the king's quartermaster. By all accounts, he was quite good at the job, so maybe? Who knew with this strange lot.

"We've been meaning to thank you," Brownbeard the Barbaric said as he stepped beside me.

I smiled. "We have, have we?"

"Yes. We have. You've done well, stowaway."

"You know that's not my real name, right?"

"It matters not. Attention, attention pirates." The pirate king again stood in front of his subjects and held up both arms. It took longer for the silence to settle in. When it did, he gestured to me.

"If he wants you to walk the plank, we have nothing to

228

worry about," Pooky said. "You jump, and I'll sit on your head."

I stood in front of the pirate king, wondering what new and strange experiences might be in store for me.

"We must now recognize one among us who is not of us, yet has served us well. We have observed that the stowaway has carried out her investigative task admirably."

Pooky sighed. "Again, with the royal *we*. Wake me up if he says anything about me. Especially if it's good, which it will be." He curled up in my arms and closed his eyes.

"I hereby bestow upon this young woman the pirate name of Stowaway Storm."

"Hurrah!"

"They're not going to let you live it down, are they?" Pooky mumbled.

"It seems not."

The king held up another arm. "And although she has not yet written her name in any ship's Pirate Codex, we feel she is in spirit one of us."

"Hurrah!"

"And on that note, we wish to invite her to sign the Pirate Codex of *The Dolphin's Kiss*."

A reverent hush settled across the crowd.

I gulped loudly. "You... you want me to join your ship as a pirate?"

"Unless you're thinking of joining my ship as a dolphin, then yes."

"What a great honor," Scotty whispered.

Quill sniffed back a tear.

"Can you tell them to keep it down? I'm trying to sleep over here."

I looked around. Everyone was watching me, mouths agape, except Tricky whose mouth was firmly clenched around her pipe's stem. Even Pepe stopped wringing out his vest to gawk.

"I thank you, your Barbaric Majesty, but my destiny lies elsewhere. I mean to go to the New World and set up a new life there, free from the constraints of the old one."

A disappointed sound rippled through the crowd. Scotty held out a palm, and several men dropped coins in it.

The king merely nodded. "I understand, Stowaway Storm. The offer is always open, if you change your mind in the future. In the meantime, let me at least bestow upon you one of the tools of a pirate. Pepe!" He snapped his fingers. "Your boots."

Pepe blanched. "But your Royal Nastiness, you gave these to me for my birthday a few months ago."

"And now I un-give them. This is the true punishment for your treachery. And of course for murdering Sweetie."

Pepe almost doubled over in his grief. He waved at the pirate behind him who was carrying his jacket, sword and boots.

The king accepted the boots from Scribbles and stepped toward me. "I believe these will fit you very well. After all, Pepe has unusually small feet for a man. Isn't that right, Small Foot?"

Sniggers broke out around us. Pepe glowered but kept quiet.

"This is a great honor," I said and gingerly accepted the boots. While Pepe might have small feet, he was taller than me, which meant the boots reached my knees. But they were beautiful boots. "I'll wear these with pride."

The king stepped back and nodded once. "Go thee well, Stowaway Storm. May the wind always be at your back, and calm seas always in front of you."

"Hurrah!"

Chapter Thirty-Five

TRICKY WAS good on her word. She didn't drop me off on an abandoned island, or trade me for camel milk, leaving me with Chief Ali Babak and his one hundred wives and concubines. Instead, she took me to the nearest port large enough to have ships setting sail for the New World.

"You're sure?" Quill asked, his eyes red-rimmed as we stood on the pier.

I glanced behind me. Strangely enough, the SS *Cedric* was here, and the captain had agreed to honor my original ticket. They'd been slowed down by an unusual storm that had bombarded London the day I left. The captain had to change the original course, sailing south for clearer, warmer waters.

"Strangest thing, miss," he'd said after handing me an updated ticket. "Unseasonal it was."

I had no doubt who caused the unseasonal storm.

I met Quill's desperate gaze. "I'm sure. I'm sticking to my plan. New World and a new life, here I come. Thank you, though. For everything."

Quill sucked in a sob, turned around and ran down the pier to the shore.

Scotty pulled me into a tight embrace. "The heart wants what the heart wants." He released me and stepped back.

Tricky nodded, rings of smoke rising faster, embers glowing fiercely in her pipe bowl. "May the wind be at your back, and calm waters ahead."

"And for you, too."

She glanced down at my knee-high boots. "This is the pirate way."

"This is the pirate way," I intoned back.

Khalid and Khalif both burst into tears, holding onto each other as if about to collapse from the weight of their emotional torrent.

"Thank you," I said. "For all the tea and great food."

"Thank them from me, too," Pooky said and twisted around the twin brothers' ankles.

"Pooky also says thank you," I said.

The brothers looked at me, at Pooky, then at each other. The crying intensified, and they staggered arm-in-arm toward the shore.

Tricky knocked a bit of ash from her pipe, watching it fall to the creaky boards. "We're hiding out in the small cove for a bit, until the sunset tide. If you change your mind..." She nodded at me, twirled around on her boot heel and marched away.

Rather than get on the SS *Cedric* right away, I strolled to the end of the pier and sat, my new boots shining in the lowering sun. Water lapped against the pillars below me. A seagull cried overhead.

"It's going to be okay," I said.

Pooky curled up on my lap. "If you say so."

"I do."

"You don't look very excited about your new life in the New World."

"It'll be fine. It's all part of the plan."

"And plans can't change?"

"Where else can I go?"

Pooky yawned and arched his back. "Wherever makes you happy."

"I'm happy."

"If you say so."

"Speaking of which, I was serious about my offer. I can arrange your passage back to London. I'm sure my step-mother'll be thrilled to see you."

Pooky looked up at me, his yellow eyes unblinking. "And who will look after you? You're constantly forgetting things. You attract trouble the way cream attracts cats, and don't get me started about your apparent insomnia. I'll have to work on my hypnosis skills with you around."

"Hmm. Because you can hypnotize people."

"Humans and witches are no match for the power of Pooky."

We sat in silence. The calm sea was awash with crimson and gold. A slight breeze trickled over the surface. It was perfect sailing weather, perfect for a pirate ship heading south.

"I'll miss those cooks," Pooky said.

"Me, too."

"And I'll definitely miss my lunches with them. What did you say they fed me?"

"Slops?"

"No. It was something far more divine than that."

"Of course. It was fillet of leftover fish."

"That's more like it."

I kicked my legs back and forth, liking the feel of the

soft leather against my feet. "These boots are definitely made for action."

"They belonged to a pirate. You think it's hygienic to use someone else's boots?"

"Sure. Less talking. More enjoying."

"You know what else I enjoyed?"

I sighed, a strange heaviness settling in my gut. "What?"

"Being with you." He turned in my lap and pressed up against me, his nose almost touching mine. "I don't want to go back to London."

"That makes two of us. What do you want?"

"A bowl of cream. I hear Khalid stole both fresh cream *and* powdered milk to make more cream. Do you think they have cream in the New World?"

"Probably not."

"It sounds terrible."

"You know what else they don't have? A pirate king."

Pooky shuddered, his tail flicking back and forth. "How uncivilized. I hear there's a pirate ship nearby."

I glanced at the horizon. The sun was just kissing the line separating sky and sea. "If we hurry, we can catch them before they set sail."

"Let's do this," Pooky said and rolled off my lap. "But you'll have to carry me. The beach has far too much of those scratchy grains."

"You mean sand."

"Dreadful stuff."

I ran down the pier, past the astonished captain welcoming passengers.

"Miss, we're leaving shortly!"

"I'm not coming!" I shouted over my shoulder.

"Again? Ticket's not refundable."

"What happens if they leave without us?" Pooky mewed in my ear.

"Less talking. More running." I veered away from the port, sprinting toward the cove where *The Pink Pearl* waited.

My boots hit the sand, and I didn't falter. Even as the surf gently rolled in, I squelched through those waves, my heart set on what was around the corner. A pink Jolly Roger. Bowls of cream. A crew of pirates.

"Can't you run any faster?" Pooky asked. "The sun's almost gone."

A stitch stung at my side, but I lengthened my stride. The beach fell away as I reached the rocky outcrop separating the port from the small cove.

I scrambled over the rocks, ignoring Pooky's hisses, and jumped off the other side, preparing to run again. I collided into Scotty.

He grinned and snapped his fingers at Clark and Stubbs. "Told you as much. Hand it over, mateys."

"Blasted barnacles!"

Clark groaned through his smile and fished out some coins.

"Yes!" Quill jumped up and down, fists in the air. "I knew it! I knew she'd come back."

I gawked at the scene. Almost the entire crew of *The Pink Pearl* were lounging on the small beach. The ship bobbed in the waters offshore, quiet and waiting.

"What're you all doing?" I stuttered.

Tricky held out her hand as Scotty placed a coin in it. "Waiting for you, apparently. It turns out you're quite useful. I just made my money back."

"When did you lose money because of me?"

Scotty grinned. "She wagered the king'd make you walk the plank. But I knew better."

Quill tried to drape his arm around me. I dodged his attempts.

Pooky stumbled past me and crawled into Khalid's arms. "I've missed you so much, cook. Please tell me you have some cream."

"Delight of my heart!" Khalid enthused and stroked Pooky. "He missed me. Let's find you some slop."

"Wait up." Tricky reached into a bag and pulled out the Codex of *The Pink Pearl*. She opened the large, battered, leather-bound book to a signing page with a list of names and signatures or fingerprints. "No non-pirates are allowed on my ship, apart from a stowaway or two. So what'll it be?"

The crew gathered around us, eyes wide. Scotty held up a coin, Clark nodded and added two.

I took the pen and glanced at Pooky, who nodded. Smiling, I wrote down our names while Tricky held the Codex for me.

My captain clamped her teeth around her pipe, puffing thoughtfully. "I hereby initiate these two fine sailors as pirates. By signing our Pirate Codex, they have now joined *The Pink Pearl* as members of the crew and our family. Stowaway Storm—"

"Hurrah!"

Tricky glanced at Pooky with a bemused look. "And Pirate Pooky, also known as Sir Dedrick Bartholomew Pocock O'Doherty the Third, descendant of the Egyptian cat goddess Bastet. Pirate Pooky, you're officially the first feline pirate in history. Congratulations to you both."

"Hurrah! Party on the ship!" My fellow pirates clapped me on the back and began to stroll toward the rowboats.

I knelt in front of Pooky. "Shall we?"

He blinked rapidly, sniffed and covered his face with a paw. "You remembered my real name."

"Of course. How could I forget a name so distinguished, regal and full of historical significance? Are you crying?"

He sat up straight and narrowed his eyes. "Cats don't cry. I have sand in my eyes. Isn't it that time of day when you feed me?"

"You mean dinnertime?"

"The name's irrelevant."

"I hear they stole some cream just for you."

Pooky purred loudly and shuffled into my arms. "And that's the pirate way."

Facts & Fiction

While the *Pirates Ahoy* series is a work of fiction, I've woven historical facts through the stories. There are also mythological elements which rest somewhere in between. Let's take a closer look, shall we?

The early real-life pirates of the Caribbean were remarkably democratic for their time. They even created a pirate republic in Nassau in the early 1700s. I decided Storm's pirates of the 1800s should retain these democratic sentiments, hence the hotly contested election for a pirate king.

While real-life pirates didn't vote for a king, they did vote for their captains. Captains were expected to be good leaders and treat their crew well. Unhappy crewmembers could call for a vote for the position of captain.

A grand conclave of pirates might've happened at some point in pirate history, although I don't think they had an annual event called the Pirate Parlay.

Each ship had its own pirate codex which each member signed when joining the crew. The codex covered a wide range of topics including distribution of wealth (it was surprisingly equitable), and punishments for various crimes.

The Kerit — also called the Nandi Bear — looks like a cross between an overgrown hyena and a bear. It's over four feet tall at the shoulder, has a steeply sloping back and a long, shaggy coat. Its favorite food is brain. If you've read Miss Knight's adventures in the *Society for Paranormals* series, you'll have already encountered the mythical Kerit on a couple of occasions.

There are more misadventures awaiting Miss Storm in the *Pirates Ahoy* series. Keep reading!

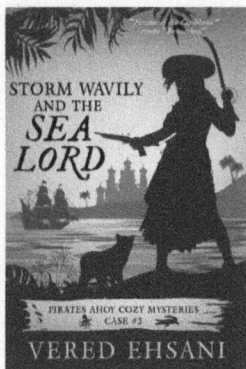

A quick favor...

Thank you for reading *Storm Wavily and The Pirate King*.

If you enjoyed this book, please consider writing a review of it on your favorite bookseller site so other readers might enjoy it too. Just a couple of sentences would mean a lot to me.

Thank you!

Vered Ehsani

About the Author

Vered Ehsani has been a writer since she could hold pen to paper, which is a *lot* longer than she cares to admit. Her work in engineering, environmental management and with the United Nations has taken her around the world. She lives in Kenya with her family and various other animals.

The monkeys in her backyard inspire Vered to create fun, upbeat adventures with a supernatural twist. She enjoys playing with quirky, witty characters who don't quite fit the template for 'normal' despite their best efforts. She's perfectly comfortable exploring the brighter side of human nature.

Are you looking for a mind-refreshing dip into a charming, fanciful world? Then welcome. Sit down with a cup of tea and prepare to be reminded that life can be a delightful place.

Write to Vered (vered@sterlingandstone.net) — she loves connecting with her readers!

Also By Vered Ehsani

* 9 7 8 1 6 2 9 5 5 3 2 0 7 *